RETURN *to* DUBLIN

AND OTHER
SHORT STORIES

Jim,
THanks for
your interest and
support.

Jack
Rosshirt

RETURN
to DUBLIN

AND OTHER
SHORT STORIES

Including six noteworthy cases of Bledsoe
Flax, Esq., a people's attorney

JACK ROSSHIRT
Author of *Kenyan Quest*

LEGACY BOOK COMPANY
A DIVISION OF GREENLEAF BOOK GROUP LP

Published by Legacy Book Company, a Division of Greenleaf Book Group, LP
4425 S. Mo Pac Expy., Suite 600, Austin, TX 78735

Submit all requests for reprinting to:
Greenleaf Book Group LP
4425 Mopac South, Suite 600
Longhorn Bldg., 3rd Floor
Austin, TX 78735
(512) 891-6100

Publisher's Cataloging-In-Publication Data
(Prepared by The Donohue Group, Inc.)

Rosshirt, Jack.
    Return to Dublin : and other short stories / Jack Rosshirt. — 1st ed.
    p. ; cm.
    "Including six noteworthy cases of Bledsoe Flax, Esq., a people's attorney."
    ISBN-13: 978-1-934541-00-5
    ISBN-10: 1-934541-00-1

1. Short stories, American. I. Title.

PS3618.O87 A6 2007
813/.6   2007929962

First Edition
Printed in the United States of America

09 08 07   10 9 8 7 6 5 4 3 2 1

Dedicated to
all Rosshirts, Killorans, Moynahans, and Hurleys
past, present, and to come.

Contents

Return to Dublin*

DUBLIN, IRELAND. NOVEMBER, 1920

- He was away when the Black and Tans fell upon his house, took his younger brother into the yard, stripped him, and beat him.
- A young lady named Molly Griffin was shot dead by the Black and Tans as she sat on her garden wall.
- A lorry load of Black and Tans, firing into a Dublin laneway, killed a girl of eight.
- Headline. "Brutal Murder by Sinn Fein. Gunfire on Sunday Morning in Dublin Cuts Down Fourteen Serving Officers in their Homes or Hotel Rooms. Some Killed before Their Wives. Five Other Murders in Cork."

Brian Mahoney had made three kills for the IRA, even though he was only 20. He looked older with his black hair, unshaven face, and long dark coat. He had started with the IRA as a messenger at the tender age of ten and had worked his way up until, in a raid on a bank, he had killed an overzealous bank guard.

*This story originally appeared in the Spring 2001 issue of Bibliophilos and appears here with their permission.

Bloodied by that killing, he carried out two subsequent assassinations. Though he considered himself working for a "holy cause," he had decided to make this his last job.

His leader, Michael Collins, agreed. Brian was on Dublin Castle's most-wanted list. The IRA wanted him out of the way before he got caught. Collins had set up a plan to get him out of Ireland after this mission.

Brian took the bus from Beara Way, where he lived with his mother and younger brother, into the central city. His Da had died in the war fighting for the British. His four older brothers and sisters had scattered to England, America, and Australia. He planned to join his brother Patrick in New York City.

The leaders agreed he could go to New York where he could raise money for the cause. He'd leave Ma alone with eleven-year-old Paddy, but life would be better for her. She could get on the dole and have enough for tea and a wee drop with her friends in the afternoon. With him gone, the Black and Tans wouldn't bother her.

He'd send money when he could. Maybe his brothers and sisters would send some too when they found out he was gone and would not be drinking up some of the money he sent.

The bus crossed the Liffey River. He got off, pulled his cap down, his coat tight, and started a long walk to make sure that no one followed. Down one street, through an alley. A look at the newspapers in the strand. A stop for tea on Nassau Street across from Trinity College, then aimlessly wandered until meeting time approached. Certain he had not been followed, he entered the pub at Custom House Quay and ordered a pint.

No one else came in. He drank half of it, then walked toward the gents'. He passed the door and went out into the alley. Three doors down he rapped on another door. It opened to a room where twenty men sat around three circular tables, giving their attention to the two men leaning against the east wall. As he took a seat, one of the other men rose and let himself out the front door, a lookout.

Brian recognized the tall man in the center, Michael Collins, the leader of the Sinn Fein War Council. Collins called for silence and then spoke briefly about recent killings. Collins had convinced the War Council that they had no chance of winning the struggle with the English until they struck a hard blow, hard enough to get the attention of Whitehall in London and to terrify their men in Dublin, including the Irish who worked for them.

He reminded the men that the Black and Tans and the British Irregulars were targeting more and more innocents. While the events appeared isolated, Collins felt convinced that the attack orders had come directly from the British out of Dublin Castle and that the "Cairo Gang," a group of British Officers who had previously served together in Egypt, lay at the heart of it all.

The gang had been reassembled in Dublin to hunt down those fighting for the Republic. The War Council decided that the Cairo Gang was the perfect target. The men in the room had been specially selected to carry out that operation. If anyone had any problems with acting, he should leave now. Not one, hard men all, moved.

Collins called the men to the side in groups of two and handed them each a slip of paper containing a target. Then the men left, one at a time. Some left out the front, some out the back. Brian returned the way he came. Once back inside the pub, he looked for the rest of his pint. Someone had already cleared it away. He ordered a half-pint and sat to watch the rain and see if the pub was being watched. He decided it wasn't, finished his beer, and left.

On the bus back home, he thought about the target he received. Tom Murphy, 234 Utton Lane. A common enough name in a common enough neighborhood. But this Tom Murphy worked for the British in Dublin Castle. Though Irish, he might as well be English for all the damage he was doing to a Free Ireland. He was a traitor. Traitors die.

Brian didn't sleep well that night. Sweat drenched him, and his arm and leg muscles twitched. His prior killings for the cause were in public places, not in a man's home. He rose before the alarm went off and dressed in the living room so as not to wake his mother or brother. He had a cup of tea. At 6:35 he pulled on his wet cap and coat, slipped the Beretta into his coat pocket, and went out to wait for the car. At the appointed time, an indistinguishable car pulled up to the curb. Brian got in. The men nodded to each other but said nothing. Each knew what they had to do. All the "appointments" with the Cairo Gang had been set at the same time, 8:00 Sunday morning.

At 7:45 Brian got out of the car one block south and one block east of the Murphy house, where the driver would pick him up after the "appointment." Brian walked north then west. He pulled his cap down tighter and gave thanks for the wet Dublin weather. As he walked south across the street from Murphy's house, he saw lights upstairs.

Getting ready for Mass, he thought. He circled a two-block area watching his time. At exactly 8:00 he went to the door and knocked.

No answer.

He knocked again, louder. In a few seconds the door opened slightly.

"Yes, what is it?" a woman's voice asked.

"I have a message for Mr. Tom Murphy from Dublin Castle."

"Give it to me."

"Sorry, I have orders to give it to him only."

"Just a moment. He's with the children. Come in."

"I'll wait here, thank you."

Shortly the door reopened. A man stood just inside in a dressing gown. A small child held his hand. "Yes, what is it?"

The child next to the man took Brian by surprise. He hesitated, then said, "Mr. Tom Murphy?"

"Yes."

"I was told to give you this." He pulled the Beretta from his pocket and shot Murphy in the chest three times.

A woman screamed.

A child wailed.

Brian walked slowly to the sidewalk.

The sound of a woman's shriek echoed in his ears. "Tom! Tom! No!"

Brian strolled unhurriedly so as to not draw attention to himself. He turned at the corner. The black car pulled up. He entered. They moved off smoothly down the street. The car took him to the Heuston Station, where the trains left for Cork, Galway, Wexford Waterford, and other points west, south, and southwest. He gave the gun to the driver and picked up a small traveling case. He walked into the station and looked at the ticket the driver had given him. The train to Cork left at 8:45. He read the newspaper until it was time to board.

He took his seat and leaned his head against the window. "Jasus, they didn't tell me about the kid." He closed his eyes and tried to sleep, but the woman's shriek, the child's wail, reverberated in his head.

At Cork, a farmer picked Brian up and took him to Skibbereen, where he spent the night in a sympathizer's home. The next day he received a change of clothing and new documentation, including a passport. He was now Timothy Hogan, a U.S. Citizen, from Chicago, Illinois.

A small fishing vessel took Tim Hogan south into that part of the Atlantic called the Celtic Sea, and then into the English channel to Cherbourg. In a few days, Tim Hogan boarded a ship to the United States and a new life.

CHICAGO, ILLINOIS, USA 1972

Kevin and John Hogan sat enjoying their after-golf beer in the men's grill of the Butterfield Country Club. "When do you think Dad's going to take the trip to Ireland we gave him?" Kevin asked.

"Damned if I know. He's the only Irishman in the whole diocese that hasn't gone back to the Ould Sod to show the relatives how rich he's gotten."

"Well. Mom's mad. She's putting on the pressure. He's seventy-three and going to check in sometime."

"Sure, but probably not soon. He's not strong but his mind's still sharp, and he still gives hell to the young lawyers. He's a cantankerous S.O.B."

"Yeah, you'd think that he'd realize we can make just as much money settling cases as trying them."

"He still practices macho law."

"Well, that's the way he built the firm, and it's what sent us all to college and supports us. Guess we should call him a lovable old curmudgeon rather than an S.O.B." John chuckled.

"I didn't think curmudgeon and S.O.B. were mutually exclusive. He didn't do bad for a mick who went to night law school."

"His friends in the department and all his Irish pals didn't hurt him any. Anyway, Mom has made all the arrangements for the trip to Ireland this August. At last count we have twenty going including Leo's newborn."

Tim Hogan, the subject of the conversation, sat nursing a Jamesons in his den in Oak Park. Bridget had gone off to visit one or more of the grandchildren, as she did most days.

After a couple of sips of the water of life, he started to reminisce, a sure sign of aging, but he also recognized it as the result of the increasing pressure to go back to Dublin. He'd avoided the memories of those times by working hard and not being able to get away. The latter was a good argument when he had a two-man law firm with five kids to support and educate. Now a figurehead, he couldn't pretend he was essential anymore.

No one knew why he didn't want to go back or why he didn't sit around bars and talk about the good old days. If they only knew. The old days brought nothing but bitter memories of poverty and the events of the last days. To him, Ireland was the small boy in the doorway. Did he get blood on him from his dad? Did he watch his Da die? Did it scar him for life? Too hard to think about. He never even confessed it, though he felt sure that some good Irish Father would give him absolution.

After a quick stop to see his brother in New York, Brian Mahoney, now Tim Hogan, had gone straight to Chicago. Despite requests, and later demands and threats, he had nothing further to do with the IRA. Michael Collins's hard tactics had eventually led to independence from England for the twenty-six counties. Collins served as the finance minister in the new government, but his bloody tactics caught up with him in 1922 when, at age 32, he was killed by other Irishmen.

The IRA lost interest in Brian. He joined the Chicago police force and buried himself in parish work and long hours doing extra duty on the force. He rose in the ranks of the police at a good clip. He eventually attended Loyola Law School night classes and graduated with honors.

His social life centered on the parish and police associates. He began to spend time with the younger sister of one of his fellow officers. In 1937 he married Bridget Phelan.

They had had a wonderful wedding at St. Dymphna's with a reception in the parish hall. After a short honeymoon in northern Wisconsin they hurried back to his busy schedule.

He sent money to Dublin for his mother. She was comfortable for the first time in her life. When she died he was "too busy" to go back for the funeral. His siblings never forgave him.

Five children came to Tim and Bridget in orderly Irish Catholic fashion: Kevin, John, Colleen, Matt, and Mary.

He passed the bar exam on the first try and left the force. His contacts got him a job in the city law department. After three years, he recognized that working for the City would not bring him the financial rewards he thought he needed for his family.

He again reached out to the Irish network in Chicago to cash in on favors he had done as a city attorney. He accepted an offer to work in the law offices of a prosperous plaintiff's attorney, Dismas Kennel. Kennel had the flashiest and most lucrative practice of any plaintiff's attorney in Chicago. Most of the large cases in Chicago ended up in his office. He didn't handle losers.

Kennel took a few smaller cases for the younger lawyers to prepare and try. By way of payment, they received a small salary and experience in the courtroom; the latter was the more valuable. Eventually the young lawyers left Kennel to strike out on their own. When they got the "big case," they called Dismas to try it. The system worked well.

Tim and Leo Tarpey, another associate at Kennel's office, opened their own office. Slowly but surely they prospered. Both were bright, hardworking, and connected. Three of Tim's children went to law school. The firm grew to twenty lawyers. Tim did less and less. He and Bridget lived at Long Beach on Lake Michigan in the summer and fall, with the kids and grandkids always welcome. Weekends there were a way of life. Tim and Bridget spent more time in the winter at one of the two condominiums he owned in Florida.

When the children brought up Tim's youth in Ireland, he referred to the Irish song where the Irishman tells his son that he doesn't talk about the old days because they were so sad.

From the few remarks Tim made, the family knew his parents had died and his brothers and sisters scattered. Their mother was different. Bridget reveled in her heritage and told them stories of growing up outside of Dublin and admitted she knew nothing of Tim's family. Bridget had gone back to Ireland many times to visit her aunts, uncles, and cousins. If she knew why Brian did not go back, she kept it to herself.

When, for Tim's seventieth birthday, Tim's children gave him, Bridget, and the grandchildren a trip to Ireland, Tim said "Thanks" but avoided any discussion of a date. Bridget and the boys kept up the pressure. Finally, Bridget laid down the law.

"Tim, you're seventy-two. God willing, you'll have many more years, but you never know. You can't go to your grave not having returned to the Holy Ground. You have to visit your mother's grave, God rest her soul. Quit being such a grump. Tim, you're going." Bridget set about making firm plans.

Tim rationalized that after fifty years, the chance of any discovery of his past had dwindled. He decided to quit resisting. But first he'd talk to his old friend, Father, now Monsignor, Paul Reagan. He called Reagan. Reagan invited him over at nine that evening when his parish obligations were over.

The two old men settled into the comfortable chairs in the priest's sitting room, a perk of age and seniority. Each had a glass of Jameson's. Tim's had ice but no water. Paul's had a little water, no ice. After a general social discussion, including comments about the fortunes of the Cubs, White Sox, Bears, and Notre Dame, the men started their second drinks.

"What brings you here, Tim?" the priest asked.

Tim took a big swig from his drink and started talking. He didn't stop, except to refill his glass, until he told Paul the whole story of his association with the IRA, the murders, and his life since he left Ireland.

When he finished, the priest said, "Tim, if the murders had happened last week, I'd tell you to go to the authorities. As it was fifty years ago, I can't see any good in ruining lives by coming forward now. Let's keep this between us and God. Would you like to treat what you told me as Confession?"

"Yes, I would," Tim said with a sense of relief.

"Are you sorry for these sins and all the sins of your past life?"

"I am."

Father Reagan said the ritual words of absolution while making the sign of the cross. "Tim, there's no penance that I could give to match what you've told me. However, to preserve form, I give you the penance of one rosary."

"Yes, Father."

"Tim, what you told me falls under the seal of confession. I'll tell no one. As a man, I'll judge you by the good life you've lived since I've known you. We'll remain friends."

"Thanks, Paul."

"Let's finish our Jameson's. Try to enjoy the trip with your family. Relax. Bring me back some Black Bush Whiskey, even though it's from the North."

THE SHELBOURNE HOTEL, DUBLIN, IRELAND, 1973

"Patrick, I need to talk to you," Sean said.

"Fine. Come on back." Patrick Murphy led the way back to his office as head of food services at the Shelbourne.

"You remember that I was around when your Dad was killed by the IRA?"

"How could I forget?" That morning had burned itself into Patrick Murphy's memory. He held his father's hand while a man shot him. The sound of the shots, the blood, and his mother's screams never left his mind. The police, the neighborhood women, and eventually the funeral all mingled together and faded, but the door opening and the shots stayed clear.

Ten years after the shooting, Patrick finished school. His family had no money for more education nor, frankly, did he have the aptitude or interest in it. A quick lad, he had good marks at the National School. His Uncle Brian, a waiter at the Shelbourne, the premier Hotel in Dublin, got Patrick a job as a busboy. He told Patrick that diligence would help him rise to waiter where he could make a fair living with the tips from the wealthy Irish, English, and Americans who stayed at the hotel. The plan sounded good to Patrick and his family, especially since jobs were not easy to come by in the 1930s.

During World War II, things grew more difficult, but Patrick , a diligent worker, kept his job and moved ahead. After the war things picked up financially. By then, Patrick had risen to senior waiter and lived a comfortable life.

As time passed, Patrick would only wake from the nightmare of his father's shooting once or twice a year. When that happened, he woke up shouting, "No! No!" and found himself sobbing. When he was in his forties, his wife suggested he see a psychiatrist.

"None of that heathen stuff for me," he declared, and that ended that.

Sean McTeague was an extra man on the bar at the Shelbourne. Though in his late seventies, he still worked during the tourist season. He helped keep the place clean, and the tourists loved his Irish accent and white beard. Sean had not always been a bartender. He had worked as a young clerk for the British and had known Patrick's father. People who worked for the British in those turbulent days kept it quiet. Patrick had a soft spot for Sean because of his connection with his father and his support for his mother after his dad's death.

Sean called Patrick over, his agitation evident.

"Calm down," Patrick said. "What's bothering you?"

"You know that big American family named Hogan that's been here seeing the sights and contacting relatives?"

"I know they exist. They're all over the place."

"The old man, the one near my age, I know him."

"Unlikely."

"Something's odd. He visits no family here. He stays in his room while everybody else goes out."

"So what? He seems pretty frail."

"I thought his staying in was strange, so one evening when they enticed him down for a drink, I took a close look at him."

"Get to the point."

"Well, you know how it is when you haven't seen a person for a long time. At first they look different, but the longer you look at them the more they look like their old self."

"I suppose so."

"The more I looked at him the more familiar his face became. Then I recognized him."

"Sean, what's this got to do with me?"

"He's Brian Mahoney. The man who shot your father."

"You're daft, man. It's been fifty years. You couldn't recognize him after half a century. You're as dotty as he is."

"Wait. Hear me out. When I worked in Dublin Castle, I was a clerk in the anti-terrorist group. We had pictures of all the assassins. I knew them by heart and hated every one of them. Unfortunately we didn't get them before the massacre. But, because of my friendship with your father, I asked to work with the team hunting for his murderer. We never got him, but we found out who he was. I had a picture of him on my desk for twenty years. We traced him to New

York then lost him. Later, when they closed the investigation, we heard rumors he had ducked out of the IRA network in New York and moved to Chicago. This Hogan is from Chicago."

"That's not enough to accuse a man of murder."

"Look. I kept a copy of the file when the official investigation closed. I looked at it last night. It's the same man."

"Sean, don't make such serious accusations on such slim suspicions."

"Patrick, I swore on your Da's grave that I'd find the man who killed him. It looks like I'm going to keep that oath."

"Turn it over to the authorities. Let them handle it."

"Nonsense. They don't care."

"Leave it alone."

"I'm going to check one more thing. If it doesn't prove out I'll drop it."

"OK, what are you going to do? No confrontations. Don't say anything about this to anyone," Patrick said. In his heart he didn't want anything to happen.

"Nothing like that. I'll let you know in a few days."

Three days later Sean came to Patrick's office. The old man sat down with a look of triumph on his bewhiskered face.

"We got him," he said.

"What do you mean?"

"I told you that I had the old file, complete with a set of fingerprints from the first time the killer was picked up in 1919. I took a glass Hogan used the other night to my grandson in the Garda lab. They match. Tim Hogan is Brian Mahoney. He killed your Dad. "

"My God. After all these years."

"Yes, and you have to do something. The Garda won't act. Even if they did, because of time and his age, they'd give him a slap on the wrist, even though he killed in cold blood."

"Let me think. Let me think. Get out. Come back in an hour. Tell Mary no calls or interruptions."

When Sean came back sixty-five minutes later, he found Patrick at his desk with his head in his hands. When Patrick looked up Sean saw wet eyes.

"It all came back, Sean. The shots, the screaming, the blood all over me when I leaned over Dad. Mom's crying. The funeral and the hard, cold days without him. Mom sad every day of her life. Even so, vengeance serves no purpose."

"It's not vengeance, it's justice. Justice for you being raised without a father, lost education, lost opportunities. Your Ma's continuous crying and that murdering bastard living it up fat and happy in Amerikay."

"What if you're wrong?"

"I'm not. The fingerprints prove it."

"They could be wrong."

"Then ask him."

"What?"

"Ask him. He sits up there in the room by himself or with the nurse and baby every day while the others are out. Go ask him."

Patrick looked at his old friend incredulously. Finally he said, "OK, I'll ask him. This afternoon. After what you told me I can't look at the man without wondering. If he convinces me you're wrong, that's it. No more talk. If he doesn't, I'll call the Garda. Let them handle it."

"All right," Sean said.

After the lunch service, Patrick checked the afternoon orders. Suite 401 wanted tea for two adults and warm milk for the baby at 4:00. Patrick told the floor waiter he'd take the tea trolley to 401.

Patrick had no idea what he'd do if this man turned out to be the man who killed his father, but he wanted to talk to him.

At ten of four he pushed the tea trolley to Suite 401. He knocked. Moira, the nanny the Hogan's had hired through the hotel, answered the door.

"Where's Paddy?" she asked, the disappointment evident in her voice.

Sounds like these two have taken a liking to each other, Patrick mused. "He's here. I serve from time to time to keep a personal hand on things and see how the guests are doing."

"We're fine. The Hogans are a grand family. They're thinking of taking me back to Chicago with them to take care of the baby. I've family there, too."

"Fine for you, Moira. I'll put your tea and the baby's milk in your bedroom. Is the old man here? I should talk to him, too."

"He's in the other bedroom. He spends most of his time reading, watching the telly, and dozing off."

"I won't disturb him. If he's asleep I'll leave the tray on his table. I'll come back in an hour to pick up."

Patrick didn't know how his talk with Tim Hogan, possibly Brian Mahoney, would go, but he didn't want to be disturbed. To help that along, he put a couple of drops of a liquid in Moira's tea. Nothing dramatic, just a little something the hotel doctor gave to the jet-lagged tourists who couldn't sleep the first few days.

Patrick pushed the tea trolley across the sitting room to the other bedroom. He knocked gently. If the man was awake he didn't want to startle him, and he didn't want to wake him if he was asleep. He wanted to do that after he was in the room. He received no answer. He opened the door. The old man lay asleep in his street clothes, on his back in bed. Patrick opened the door and pushed the trolley through. The old man didn't look like most of the rich Irish-Americans who stayed at the hotel. They were mostly overweight, with red faces and silver gray hair, Hogan a.k.a. Mahoney had a thin, long, well-creased face, and very little hair on his head. The hair that remained was dark gray and stringy. Patrick gently shook the man.

"What? What?" Hogan sputtered. He looked up through a sleepy haze.

"A moment please, Mr. Mahoney."

"What? Who the hell are you?" His eyes focused. "The waiter! Jesus Christ, I'm trying to sleep. Leave the damn tea and get out of here."

"Are you Brian Mahoney?"

Concern entered the man's just-opened eyes. Warily he looked at Patrick. "I'm Tim Hogan and if you don't get the hell out of here, I'll have your ass fired."

"I don't think so, Brian Mahoney. I think you're the man that shot my father while I held his hand fifty years ago. Look at me and tell me you're not."

The blood drained from Mahoney's face as he sat up now with his legs over the side of the bed. He anchored his left hand to the nightstand. "You're crazy. Is this some kind of demented Irish joke? I was born and raised in Chicago. I'm calling security. When I am done with you, you'll wish somebody had shot you."

"I didn't come here to harm you. I just came to see how a man could live with murder on his soul for fifty years."

As the old man pushed himself up he slipped. He gripped the nightstand to steady himself. As the man sagged, Patrick instinctively grabbed his arm to support him.

"Let go of me you son of a bitch," Hogan yelled hysterically. He swung his free hand up and slapped Patrick across the face. Though a weak blow, it stung. Patrick's hand went to his face. His adrenaline flowed. "I just want to talk to you," he said.

As Patrick's grip tightened, Hogan picked up a Waterford crystal ashtray from the nightstand and hit Patrick above the ear. The pointed edge punctured the skin, stunning Patrick. He staggered backward. In a frenzy, Hogan hit Patrick again, drawing more blood.

The savagery of the attack and the blood flowing down the side of his face inflamed Patrick. He threw himself at the old man. Mahoney was no match for his weight. Patrick pushed him down on the bed, circled his throat with his hands and squeezed until his savagery subsided.

Still manic, Patrick stood and looked down at the old man as he lay on the bed with his hands and arms extended as if on a cross. He was dead.

Patrick sank into a chair. "Oh my God. Oh my God." Then a thin smile came over his face. "I've done it. Justice." Hyperventilating, he got up. "We're not even *yet*." He threw the man's feet up on the bed and hurried through the sitting room to the other bedroom door. He wiped some of the blood from his face and onto his pant leg. He opened the door slowly. Moira sat asleep in her chair, a book in her lap.

"Justice has been done, now vengeance."

He walked to the double bed and picked up a pillow. He crept to the crib. "The sins of the father are visited on the sons. Let Hogan's family suffer like my mother and I suffered."

He lowered the crib side and took the pillow in both hands. The baby had not moved. He lay on his back with his tiny hands and arms extended like his grandfather's two rooms away. Curly blond hair framed a pink face that Patrick presumed included blue eyes. The baby breathed regularly through its small, bowed, open mouth.

Patrick reached down with the pillow. His mind, still whirling, remembered the Bible quote: "Vengeance is mine; I will repay."

He let go of the pillow with his right hand. The hand went to the baby's throat. How small. His thumb felt the tiny but steady pulse in the throat. The hand moved to the sleeping baby's head. With his thumb he made the sign of the cross on the child's forehead. *Pax vobiscum*, peace be with you.

Patrick dropped the pillow, walked over to the phone, and called security.

Death on Aran Island

"Maria, get Falcone in here—now!" Donatti barked into the inter-
com.

Five minutes later Falcone stood in front of his agitated boss, Sal
Donatti, who held a red, bound audit report.

"Is this right?" Donatti asked, shaking the report at Falcone.

"Yes, sir."

"This says that Kelly was skimming over $500 a week from our
confidential funds the last two years. That right?

"Right."

"And before that?"

"We don't know. We haven't gone back any further. He only left a
few months ago, and we don't audit the confidential accounts every
month. Besides, he was responsible for the audit before he left."

"You mean we don't watch the auditors. What kind of business
practice is that?"

"We've got to cut it off somewhere. We have to trust someone."

"Goddam mick. Shouldn't have hired outside the family."

"Jesus, Boss. That was thirty years ago."

"Yeah, and the only reason we did it then was because his mother and my mother were both in the Altar Society at St. Anthony's. Crap. How much more do you think he took?"

"No idea. Could be thousands. He handled all the skimmed cash we sent out for laundering."

"Where is he?" Donatti barked.

"Don't know. We sent a couple guys to his house. The neighbors said he went on a vacation. Said he was going to spend a few days driving down the coast then flying to Ireland."

"Family?"

"His wife died five years ago. His son died last year in a car crash a week after his college graduation. Nobody else."

"Tough. OK. Don't screw around. Call Dino and get someone on it. Get the money and him. Especially him. You know what happens if word gets out you're soft."

"Yes, Boss."

"Dino?" Falcone said into the phone.

"Whose callin'?"

"Joe Falcone."

"And?"

"Need to talk to you."

"Too early."

"Right away."

"Hey, I'm a late sleeper."

"Boss says now. Meet me at the Papa's Diner in forty-five minutes."

"Jeeze."

"Don't disappoint Sal."

An hour later Dino walked into Papa's. He spotted Falcone in the back booth eating donuts.

"Hey, they'll think you're a cop with those donuts," Dino said as he slid into the booth. He signaled the waitress for coffee. "What's up?"

"Emergency. An ex-employee retired with more in his retirement fund than he was untitled to. The boss wants it back."

"Details?"

"All you need to know, description, history are in this envelope. The bad news is he's disappeared. His neighbors say he's on his way to Ireland."

"Has he left the country yet?"

"Don't think so. We checked the flights out of New York and Newark. No reservations, but we found him booked on a flight out of Atlanta."

"So he is gone."

"No, he's still in Atlanta. In your package you'll find two tickets for an afternoon flight to Atlanta connecting to Shannon. Got a passport?"

"A couple of them." Dino said over his coffee cup. "But, I don't think I can do the business."

"The boss says you can."

"OK, OK. Give me the stuff. If I can't do it I've got someone who can. Usual fee?"

"More. The usual fee and expenses plus ten percent of what you get back."

"Got it. Call you when I get something. Here, pay my bill on the way out."

Jim Kelly's family had its roots in County Galway so he planned to go first to Galway City, drive out and around Connemara, up to Donegal and, finally, down for a few days in Dublin. After that it was open.

At 6:30 p.m. he plunged into the packed humanity in the Atlanta airport. Two hours before departure time, he was at the check out counter with over two hundred people. He checked in, went through security, found a seat in the waiting area, and started on a police procedural by Bartholomew Gill set in Dublin. He thought it an easy and appropriate way get into the culture.

After a few minutes he put the book down and looked at the crowd. It was the height of the vacation season both in Ireland and the States. The waiting room had a full quota of red-faced, silver-haired American men taking their families back to the Ould Sod and Irish families returning from visiting their relatives and, in one case he overheard, Disneyland.

The usual businessmen in their ties and jackets filled out the crowd, and there were a few people he could not label, like the two men in dark sport coats and open-collared shirts, noticeable because of their sunglasses. They looked like businessmen but carried no briefcases or laptops, just smallish carry-on bags with wheels. Then of course he noted the usual gaggle of students with backpacks.

The plane started loading. Jim found his window seat halfway down the plane in the 2-5-2 configuration. He watched the other passengers trying to jam their fat carry-ons in the overhead bins, and the families with kids, who had most of the middle sections, fighting over where each child would sit.

The two men in the sunglasses passed Jim on their way to the back of the plane. Did they look at him especially or had he imagined it?

He remembered what his neighbor said when he called them to check on whether the gas was off about two men coming to ask about him. Had Falcone or Donatti discovered something?

As Jim adjusted his books, earphones, and pillow, a young man, after a few tries, managed to force his backpack into the bin over his seat.

"Excuse me, I think that's my seat by the window," the young man said.

"Don't think so." A check of the ticket stubs revealed the young man had the aisle seat.

The young man's sandy hair, hanging slightly over the collar, light Celtic coloring, and body build reminded him of his dead son, Pat. Father and son were never close and it was even worse after his wife died. In fact he never had the chance to tell Pat about the nest egg he had saved for retirement and had planned to pass on to Pat when the time came.

During the meal, after a little relaxing wine, the seatmates started to chat.

During the course of their conversation, Jim told the boy he had just retired, was widowed, and was going to Ireland to visit a couple of weeks. He never mentioned that he didn't plan to return.

"Glad to know you. The name here is Sean Murray. Just finished my second year at Georgia Tech but had to drop out because of lack of money. I guess I could have gotten loans but I didn't want to start out life with over $40,000 in debt. Thought I'd hike around Ireland before starting a job in Florida."

In turn, Jim told Sean about his son, and that Sean put him in mind of him. After a while they dozed off in the darkened cabin.

The next morning, the plane landed at Shannon in a soft rain. The passengers moved through the immigration line quickly. Jim noticed the officials in the booth were dressed informally, a more welcoming sign than a uniformed functionary.

As they stood at the baggage carousel, Jim said, "It looks a typical wet Irish day out there, a little damp for hiking. Let me give you a ride to Galway. I'm going to spend a day there, then go west to Carraroe and get the boat out to the Aran Islands. You're welcome to come as far as you want."

"Thanks, I want to hike, see the countryside and meet people, but I won't do much of either in this rain, so I'll take you up on your offer."

"Good. I'll meet you over by the rental desk after I get my bags and change a little money."

The two met at the Hertz desk and carried their bags across the road to slot 46 where they threw their luggage into the small boot in the rented Micra. With warnings aplenty to drive on the left side of the road, they started off down the "wrong side" in the light rain.

The men spoke off and on as they drove slowly, commenting on the countryside and travel plans.

"Look, Sean, if you're going into Connemara you ought to see the Aran Islands. You can go with me to the island and then head up to Clifden and around to Donegal on your own."

"Thanks, let me think about it. I'll read up about the islands in *The Lonely Planet,* and if they're as interesting as I've heard I'll join you."

"Fine. I'm staying at the Great Southern Hotel in Galway City. I'll let you off downtown at Eyre Square, and you can ask about a hostel. If you want to go with me, leave a message at the hotel. I'll probably leave the day after next.

"Appreciate the offer. I'll be in touch."

Jim checked in to the old Great Southern with its high ceilings and oriental rugs. He took a bath in the large tub and crawled into the oversized bed for a nap. When he woke up about 3:00, he felt hungry. He skipped O'Flaherty's Pub in the basement of the hotel deciding to stretch his legs.

A walk around Kennedy Park, with the statue of the American president, got his blood moving a little. He spotted the Skeffington Hotel and Pub on the south side of the square and entered. The interior, with its large paneled walls and polished banisters, had many small, cozy areas. He took a seat and ordered a pint of Guinness and a roast beef sandwich from the carvery. As he was finishing the sandwich and nursing his pint, he looked around at the ornate carvings. Only then did he notice the two fellow travelers from the plane eating lunch. They had changed into black jackets and slacks but still wore their dark glasses. And while they ate their lunch, neither seemed intent on conversation.

Jim finished his pint and left by the rear entrance. The alley took him to the walking street interestingly called Shop Street. As he strolled down the street toward St. Nicholas Cathedral and the Eason Book Store, he couldn't help glancing back to see if he could spot the "dark men" as he now thought of them.

He didn't see them. The rest of the afternoon and evening passed pleasantly as he checked off the obligatory tourist sights. He slept well.

When he returned to the hotel the next day at noon from his morning sightseeing, he found a note from Sean that said, "I'll take you up on your offer of a ride. See you at 3:00."

At 3:15 they pulled into the traffic and followed the signs to Salthill and Spidal. They rolled through the amusement area with the chip shops, pubs, and entertainment houses. The sandy beach and Galway Bay were on the left.

Eventually the buildings thinned, and the land on the right flattened to the rocky ground that typified Connemara.

At Rossaveal they turned left and drove the short distance to the harbor. They booked two places on the 10:00 boat the next morning to Inishmor, the largest of the Aran Islands. The sporadic but friendly conversation in the car had resulted in Sean's concession that he'd like to see the island and would accept the invitation to spend the night with Jim in his rental cottage.

The morning dawned with untypical clarity. At 9:45, Jim and Sean boarded the boat. After the short, uneventful trip, they disembarked and started the ten-minute walk, past the crowd of horse cart drivers, to the center of Kilronan. As they stopped to bargain with one of the drivers, the two dark men in their black jackets and baseball caps walked by them.

"Wait," Jim said.

"What?"

"The two guys in black."

"What about' em?"

"They were on the plane and they were in the restaurant in Galway."

"Geez, there are hundreds of tourists."

"I think they're following me."

"Why would they do that?"

"I have a reason."

"What?"

"Nevermind."

Jim tried to put the suspicions out of his mind, but he kept thinking back to the men who visited his house and his "nest egg." While Jim fretted, Sean bargained with one of the cart drivers over the price of a pony cart trip to the Dun Aengus, the fort high on the cliff dropping down into the Atlantic on the south side of the island.

Negotiations concluded, they climbed into the wooden cart, and the pony plodded across the undulating limestone reef that was the island. Nature had created a moonscape, with sheets of gray rock and massive boulders punctuated by bits of flowers and grass pushing their way up here and there. They saw endless man-made patches of grassy land where, over hundreds of years, the land had been cleared by hand and fertilized by the farmers with seaweed. But nothing went to waste. The farmers had used the rocks to build the walls around small fields.

Halfway to the fort they saw clouds starting to build up over the mainland. By the time they reached the buildings at the start of the walk to the fort, a mist had begun to gather.

"Should we go up?" Jim asked.

"Certainly," the driver said. "You didn't come all this way not to see the fort."

Sean agreed, and the two men started the eight-hundred-yard walk up the rock and grass incline to the 2,000 year-old fort.

The men unpacked their anoraks and put them on as a light mist settled over them. By staying on the grass as much as possible, they soon reached the defensive circle of sharp stones that protected the fort proper. As they started through the small entrance in the looming stone wall, the two dark men emerged. Jim immediately thought they must have taken one of the mini buses up.

Passing through the narrow opening, they entered into a large, grassy area inside the half circle of massive stone walls. While most of the literature referred to the structure as a fort, some viewed the edifice as a ceremonial theater. Whatever it had been, the other half of the wall offered an abrupt drop off, about 200 feet into the ocean.

"Sean, look around. I think I'll have chat with those guys that just came out," Jim said.

"What for?"

"Just curious. I'll just be minute."

Jim went back out the door and looked around. The two men hadn't started down but had walked in the other direction to the cliff's edge and appeared to be trying to taking pictures of the escarpment as it extended dramatically as far as the eye could see. It seemed an unrewarding task as the mist had degenerated into to a persistent rain.

"Hello," he said as he approached them.

"Hello," the man with camera the responded.

"Saw you on the plane."

"Possible."

"Saw you in Galway," Jim said with an edge in his voice.

"We were there. You gotta problem?"

"Are you following me?" Jim asked

"Are you nuts? Why would we do that? Bug off."

Jim picked up a New Jersey accent. His hands began to shake. His heartbeat accelerated. The rain had grown heavier, and water dripped off the men's clothing, gathering in little pools over the surface of the rough rock on which they stood.

"Are you from Donatti?" Jim asked.

"Never heard of him."

"Well, just leave me alone."

"You're alone, buddy. You'd better see your shrink when you get back to the States."

With fist clenched, Jim yelled, "Quit following me."

"You're nuts. Get out of here," the other man ordered.

Jim spun around to leave. His left foot tripped over one of the jagged rocks. His right foot slipped on the wet surface. He went down hard to all fours.

The man without the camera reached down to steady him and help him up. Jim felt the hands grip him. Hysterically he swung his right arm back and up to shake off the offending grasp. He struck the would-be Samaritan in the face. The man staggered back and slipped on the rain-slick rocks. As he waved his arms trying to catch his balance, his companion reached for him. He missed, and instead gave him a slight push.

Slight as the contact was, it was enough to upset the delicate balance of the man he had been trying to preserve, and he skidded over the two-hundred-foot precipice to the rocks below.

"Tony! Tony!" the man yelled just before jumping after his friend.

Jim fainted.

"Jim, Jim you ok?" Sean said as he shook him.

Jim's eyes opened slowly but his mind raced. What happened? Stay calm. Keep quiet, he thought.

By now the rain came down harder, making seeing even a short-distance difficult.

"I'm ok. I guess slipped and hit my head."

"Lucky you weren't closer to the cliff."

"Yes. Help me up."

"What happened to the guys you were going to talk to?"

"They were gone when I came out," Jim said quickly.

They slipped and slid down to the waiting pony cart in the heavy rain, wishing they had taken a minivan. The men huddled in miserable silence in the back of the cart. The driver, and the pony, took the rain in stride. When they got to town, Jim headed for the pub and downed a couple of whiskeys to quell his shivering while they waited for the boat to depart.

Back at the cottage, after a bath and more whiskey, Jim fell asleep until about 11:00 when he woke to find Sean sitting in front of the peat fire reading.

"Do you want to tell me what happened out there?" Sean asked.

Jim had been laying in bed trying to figure out what to do. Donatti was after him and the money. Now this disaster. If they were Donatti's men, he'd send more. He thought he had a plan.

Jim told Sean about the money and what happened on the cliff. Neither man could make any sense out of it.

"I believe they're hunting me down. I only wanted some money for my old age."

Sean listened attentively. "So what now?"

"We'd better separate for your sake. I'll take you to Clifden tomorrow, and you can continue your trip before they tie you in with me."

"Fine."

"Something else. They'll run me down sooner or later, but they don't have to get the money."

"Why not?"

"Because it's in a confidential account with the Bank of Ireland."

"I thought those were in Switzerland."

"Ireland had them until a short while ago. I opened the account before the laws changed."

"If they catch you, they'll force you to tell."

"Maybe, but not all of it. I told you that you remind me of my dead son. It's corny, but I'd like you to have some of the money. I'll give you a draft on the account for $40,000. Take it and use it for your education."

The older man and the younger man exchanged protests and insistences until they went off to bed. The matter seemed settled. After breakfast, Jim drove Sean through the countryside to Clifden and let him off in the city square outside the Clifden House Hotel. Jim handed Sean a written direction to the bank to pay to Sean $40,000 with the account number on it.

"I'm glad you agreed to take the money," Jim said. "It'll make me think I did something for my son."

"Thank you very much. I'll try to do well to honor your son. Oh, and I don't think those men were after you but be careful."

"I will." Jim started to drive the seventeen miles to the next tourist sight, Kylemore Abbey.

No sooner had Jim pulled away than Sean walked across the square to the Bank of Ireland branch office. He asked for the manager and presented his handwritten draft. After a number of phone conversations with the head office in Dublin, a fax of the letter to Dublin to check the signature, and a thorough review of Sean's passport and other identification, the bank manager gave him a bank draft for the Irish pound equivalent of US$40,000.

Sean walked back across the square and checked in. Once in the room, he called Newark and recorded a message on an answering machine.

"This is Angelo. Tell Sal I got part of his money back. The rest is in a 'secret' account with the Bank of Ireland." He read off the account number that had been on the letter. "Sal's banking connections should be able to get the rest. Kelly's probably going to be occupied with the Irish police for a while."

The next day, Angelo waited for his plane back to the States from Shannon Airport. Before he went through security, he went to a phone booth and made an anonymous call to the Garda in Galway. He told them to look for an American tourist named Jim Kelly who had information about the recent deaths on the Aran Island of Inishmor.

A week later, the *Irish Times* carried a story under the headline "Garda Investigates Possible Hate Crime in Aran Islands."

Part of the story read, "An American is assisting police in the investigation of the death of two American tourists who fell to their deaths off a cliff on the Aran Island of Inishmor last week. Sources close to the investigation indicate that it is believed the two men were homosexuals who were making a pilgrimage around Europe. It is possible that one of the men had AIDS. The connection between the man helping the police and the deceased is not known. Police spokesmen refuse to comment except to confirm that the investigation into the deaths is ongoing."

Big Bully

Percy Robert's teeth banged against the spout of the water fountain. It hurt. Not as much as when really smashed down, but it still hurt. The bang didn't crack the porcelain of his teeth. That would bring down the wrath of his mother and the principal. But it still hurt and made Percy mad.

Three times this month, they'd pushed his head down when he took a drink. He usually tried to back up to the water fountain and take a quick sip, but even then they caught him.

This wasn't the only way Percy's classmates harassed him. And why not? He made the perfect target for seventh-grade boys exercising their flowering masculinity and natural cruelty. Shorter than most of his classmates, fifteen pounds overweight, protruding teeth, red hair, and glasses all combined with nature to put a permanent "kick me" sign on Percy. Add to that his name and the facts that he did his assignments, answered in class, got all "A"s and didn't play sports, and you'd wonder how he survived this long.

Normally a short, fat, funny-looking boy could get along with a minimum of abuse by sinking into the woodwork. Such a retiring misfit might get picked on only once or twice a week. But if such a person spoke up every day in every class, it added a "Hit me, I'm smart" sign under the "Kick Me" invitation.

In fact, his classmates had picked on Percy so much and so easily, the biggest bullies in the class, Fred and Mike, grew bored with it and delegated the harassment of Percy to their underlings, especially Bill and Tom, thugs in training. These more averaged-sized seventh graders happily took up the persecution by knocking his books off the desk, shoving him in the hall, salting his food at lunch, and heckling him on the playground. Other kids avoided Percy so they wouldn't feel the fallout.

Although Bill and Tom more closely matched Percy's size than the others, he had lost the will to fight back. Not playing sports meant that he possessed less strength than his antagonists. He also felt that if he did fight back, Fred and Mike—the really big guys— might return and do him no good.

Finally, Bill and Tom got bored just harassing Percy in school. "Let's beat him up," Bill suggested. "Then he won't answer so quickly in class."

"Whaddya mean?" Tom asked.

"A little pushing and shoving amounts to nothing. He enjoys it. Let's put a little hurt on him and tell him he'll get more if he doesn't shut up in class."

"Right. Then he'll know that Fred and Mike aren't the only tough guys in school."

"OK, but we can't do it here. The teachers will break it up."

"Let's wait for him after school. He takes the shortcut through the big lot off Willow Street. He usually does some sissy stuff in the classroom after school. We can get him alone about 4:30."

"Thursday's a good day—no ball practice after school. I'll start the fight. You jump in."

Word of the pending "fight" shot throughout the class. On Thursday at 4:15 Tom and Bill sat behind the tree next to the path.

Ten or twelve of their buddies scattered around the edge of the lot behind bushes and trees, waiting for the show.

Sure enough, Percy stayed after school. About 4:20, his book bag over his right shoulder, he walked the two blocks to Willow and started on the diagonal path across the large lot—really two city blocks. All the kids who lived northwest of school took this shortcut.

Percy had walked about a third of the way along the path when Bill stepped from behind a tree.

"Hey Percy. Whatcha been doing? Kissing some teacher's ass?"

Percy kept walking. "No, just helping out."

"Yeah, we know how you get all those "A"s. Brownnosing."

"No, I study. You should try it."

Now only a few feet separated the two boys. Percy swerved left to ease around Bill. Bill jumped right to block his way.

"Don't smart-mouth me, asshole," Bill said as he slugged Percy in the right shoulder.

"I didn't," said Percy. He slid his book bag in front of himself as a shield. He countered right to avoid Bill, but Tom stepped from behind the tree blocking that move.

Now Percy faced two antagonists. His gut told him to dash between them. Holding his book bag in front, he tried to rush through. Both boys shoved him back, hard. Percy stumbled but kept his feet.

"Ya know, Tom, Percy needs a little smack to let him know he can't push into us."

"Right."

"Why'd you push us, Percy?"

Tom slammed his fist into Percy's left shoulder.

"I didn't. I just want to go home."

"Want to see Mommy?"

Bill hit him in the other shoulder.

Quietly the other boys formed a circle around the three.

"Want to do your homework?"

"No, I've got to help my mother."

"Wow, he's not only a kiss-ass in school, but he's mommy's little helper."

Bill hit Percy in the nose. His glasses flew off. Percy dropped his book bag and felt his face. His hand came away bloody.

With the bag down, Tom hit him in the stomach. Percy bent over and started to whimper. The crowd murmured and moved their arms in hitting motions, clenching and unclenching their fists.

Percy picked up his bag. Holding it in front of him, he faced off against Bill. Tom edged around to the back of Percy. Tom uncorked a round house swing that caught Percy solidly on the head above his right ear.

"Yeah, get him!" several in the crowd yelled.

Percy staggered and dropped to one knee. Pain stabbed his temple. It also unleashed a tremendous flow of adrenaline. Water filled Percy's eyes, but he could still see Bill standing in front of him smirking.

Instinctively Percy surged up and forward and grabbed Bill by the neck. The intensity of the charge and Percy's extra weight knocked Bill to the ground. Percy straddled Bill, pinning Bill's arms down with his knees. Percy heard animal sounds come from his throat. He held Bill's neck with his left hand and slammed his right hand back and forth across Bill's face.

"Bastard, bastard, bastard," he said as he wildly swung. After the first blows, the swings turned rhythmic. Slap! Slap! Slap! Blood and mucous covered Bill's face.

The bloodlust of the crowd now made them encourage Percy. Tom tried to pull Percy off but the ferocity of the attack scared him away. In his frenzy Percy hardly noticed the pulling at his shoulders. Suddenly, stronger arms pulled at Percy.

"What are you doing? Get off, get off!" a woman shouted. Bill's mother, coming back from the store, had seen the fight and recognized Bill's red jacket. "Billy, Billy, what has he done to you?" Kneeling down, she wiped the mess off his face.

Percy picked up his bag. Someone handed him his glasses as he pushed his way through the crowd. No one stopped him. A voice said, "Good fight, Perc." He got a couple of pats on the back.

Ten yards down the path he heard Bill's mother yell, "Percy Roberts, I'm going to call your mother and the school principal! You're nothing but a big bully, a big bully."

Percy stopped. What did she say? A big bully?

He wiped blood and sweat from his face with the back of his sleeve. His breathing slowed and a smile crossed his face. As the smile expanded into a grin, he started running so that he could get home quickly and get bawled out by his mother for turning into a big bully.

Fear

"God damn it. Why don't they die?" Seth said as he banged his coffee cup on the table. The coffee sloshed over his pie and silverware.

"How dare you? God will punish you." Ruth replied. "The Bible says honor thy father and mother. That doesn't mean just when they're young and healthy. That means when they're in their eighties, too."

"Can it. Your Bible group just doesn't live in the real world. Mom's fought cancer for five years and Dad has had three heart attacks. It's time."

"God decides the time. I know you're under a lot of stress. You need some serious help. You're not yourself."

"I need money. That's what I need. I'm getting nasty calls and letters every day. They're even calling me at work. The boss said to get it settled or I could be out on my ass."

"I thought your friend offered to help."

Seth didn't answer her question. Then he said, "Their house isn't worth much, but the lot's worth a bundle. They paid the mortgage off years ago."

"That house means everything to them. They raised you and your sister in it. They have friends in the area, and go to church nearby. They're comfortable."

"Crap. No one knows them anymore. The people who tore down and built the houses on either side of them call the folks' house an eyesore. The neighbors wouldn't know them if they fell over them, which they might do someday."

"Seth, I can't stand it when you're like this. When did you get so greedy? Get some help. I'm going to the church to prepare food baskets."

"You don't help any with all your donations to your church and all those goody-two-shoes organizations."

"The Bible says feed the poor. I'm doing what God wants me to do. You should, too. Anyway, you're supposed to go see your folks this evening—it's Wednesday. Try to treat them nicely."

"It's useless, but I'll go see them. I'll probably stop at the club on the way back. Don't wait up."

"The club. That's an expense we don't need. And the bar bills."

"Damn it, don't get started."

Ruth picked up her bag and rushed out the back door before she got any angrier. I should talk to Pastor Dobbs about this, she thought.

Seth cleaned up the wet mess and poured himself more coffee.

That evening, he pulled up in front of the modest, one-story house in the recently gentrified neighborhood. Its proximity to downtown made it a developer's dream. Seth sat and looked at the light in the front window. He remembered the lamp, a gift from his late aunt Grace. It cast a dim glow on the ugly green and blue drapes that had hung there for at least forty years.

Until a few years ago, the house brought back pleasant memories of neighborhood friends, the local school, and pickup ball games in the vacant lots. No vacant lots now. Builders tore down the other modest homes and built big houses, leaving little green space. Like the old houses, his parents should make way for the new, he mused.

Sighing, he went up to the front door and rang the bell to give a warning. With his key he unlocked the door and let himself in. At the sound of the bell, his father John, who could still hear well, reached for his walker, pulled himself up, and started shuffling to the door.

After Mary had finished her chemo and came home, the old couple had taken out a reverse mortgage. With the money, they had the second bedroom and old den made into one large area. Now it was a combined family room and hospital space. A hospital bed and Mary's medical equipment dominated one side of the room. They placed the bed so that Mary could look at the flowers and trees in the small backyard that a man came to care for once a week—the couple's only extravagance. On the other side of the room, a good-sized TV set allowed John to sit in his lounge chair near the bed and watch sports, and Mary to see her news and family programs. Their failing eyesight and inability to concentrate for long periods without falling asleep limited their once avid reading. Even large type books didn't help much.

Seth got to the room door before his Dad did. "Hi, Dad. I told you before you didn't have to let me in."

"Need the exercise," the old man joked.

Seth gave a perfunctory hug to his dad, walked over to the bed, and gave his mom a kiss. As he entered the old front door he remembered entering hundreds of times, coming home from school to a warm hug and offers of food, which he usually declined because he had to change out of his school togs and get into baseball gear. For a moment, he remembered a time when he was a better person.

"Get a beer from the kitchen and sit down and visit," John said.

"OK." Seth, having made the trip to the fridge a hundred times, did it again. "Can't stay long," he said when he returned with the beer.

John and Seth chatted about sports, but John talked mostly about old teams and players that Seth had little knowledge of. Mary smiled. It reminded her of pleasant times.

Seth's sister Betty called once a week from the next state. She told the old folks about her two children, now in their late twenties. Mary passed on to Seth the news of his nieces. Seth and Mary rarely talked. The visit passed slowly.

When he finished his beer Seth said, "Gotta go."

"Thanks for coming by. See you next week," John said.

"Sure, Dad. Ruth will pop in this weekend to see if you need anything. Bye, Mom," he said as he leaned over the bed and gave her a kiss on her forehead.

"I'll walk you out," John said.

"No need, Dad." It'll take forever, he thought.

"Got to," his dad replied.

There was new furniture in the back room, but the living room furniture and rugs all had seen better days in another era. While not shoddy, their wear showed. All had a musty odor about them. John slumped down in the nearest chair.

"I've got to go, Dad."

"Your drink'll wait. Sit down." The old voice took on a bite it did not have earlier.

Seth sat. "What?" he snapped.

"First, your mother's in a lot more pain than she let's on. She uses a lot of pills."

"Sorry."

"Secondly, your mother and I have talked about lending you money to pay your bills. We can't do it."

"Sure you can. You can sell the house."

"Maybe we can, but we won't. You're a grown man. You have got to handle your own finances."

"Why not sell? It's worth a small fortune. You could move in to a home, lend me what I need, and have plenty to live on."

"No. We're comfortable here. We don't want to live stacked up with a lot of other old folks like cord wood, waiting to die." The old man's voice trembled.

"Dad, I really need the money."

"I know. I got a call from some fellow about you and your money problems. I think he threatened me. I hung up on him."

"Sorry," Seth said halfheartedly.

"Sell one of those fancy cars and the boat. Sell your house." John said unsympathetically.

"Dad, I'm entitled—"

"You're entitled to nothing." John's hands shook and he leaned forward in his chair.

"Your mother and I lived frugally, sent you to good schools. You're entitled to nothing more. If you can't manage your affairs, it's your problem."

"Dad."

"I'm not finished. You've handled your money poorly. We can't put ourselves in your hands. Old people fear a lot of things. Like losing independence. Loss of health we can't do much about, but we can fight against loss of financial independence. Asking your eighty-year-old parents to support you. What a laugh. If you can't help us at least don't make this worse. "

This jolted Seth. He didn't remember his parents ever rejecting him before. The old folks seemed his last chance. It scared him, then injected venom into his system.

"All right, old man. But you'll regret this," he said angrily as he rose.

"Seth, wait." John struggled to get out of his chair.

"No, you wait." He moved in front of his father. Towering over him, he fumed, "I need money and I need it now and I'm going to get it." With that he shoved the old man back toward the chair and turned. He had pushed his father harder than he had intended and the feeble old man could not catch hold of the chair arm. He crumpled to the floor. Seth had seen none of the results of his push, as he had bolted out the door.

John told Mary about the confrontation but not about the push. "I've never seen him like that," John said. "It's like he's having a breakdown. Does debt do that to people?"

"There must be something more," Mary said. "You think he'll get violent? Maybe he'll hurt us to get the money like you see on TV?"

"No. I don't think so."

However, the more they talked about going into a home, the more their worry grew. Suddenly, they feared the future.

Seth looked up from the martini glass into the face of the smiling, relaxed man in the golf shirt across the table from him. "Look, Mel. I'll get you the money. I just talked to my parents and they'll loan it to me," Seth lied, "but it takes time to do the paperwork with the bank."

"OK, but the vigorish is mounting up. Every week you owe a grand more. Even then I can't let somebody welsh on me. Hurts my reputation in the community. I'll give you ten days."

"Alright, but don't call my folks or the office any more."

"Oh we're past that. I'll send somebody over to your house next Wednesday evening for the money."

"Yeah, fine," Seth murmured.

To end the harassment from his legion of creditors, Seth had borrowed enough from Mel to pay them all off. Mel was the buddy of Joe, a friend at the country club. Over drinks one night, Joe told him that Mel had advanced money to him and to a lot of other club members who found themselves in a tough spot. When approached in the club bar, Mel quickly agreed to lend Seth the money. Seth thought it odd that Mel had done it on a handshake, no loan papers involved. Mel said he always did business that way—quick, no lawyers. Anyway, Seth had no choice, because any legitimate lender wouldn't touch him because of his bottom-of-the-ocean credit rating. Even the loan consultants who advertise on TV and send e-mails wouldn't lend to him.

Only later did Seth discover what kind of a bad deal he had made. Mel computed the interest, which had seemed reasonable, weekly instead of annually. Seth got a queasy feeling in his stomach when he thought of it. The booze helped a little, but he grew more fearful as the days passed.

Bemused by both the drink and his desperate situation, Seth stumbled his way to his car at the edge of the country club parking lot. He pushed the key alarm to unlock the door.

"Seth," a voice said. Seth looked around and saw two bulky men come around the car parked next to his.

"Do I know you?" Seth asked as he tried to focus his eyes in the dimness.

"Not yet. We are friends of Mel and have a message for you."

"What? I just talked to him in the bar."

"Well, he didn't want to give you this message there." Then the first man pinned Seth's shoulders against the side of his car. The second man took something from his jacket and hit Seth twice across his right knee with it.

Seth screamed and dropped to the ground, holding his knee.

"You broke my knee," he moaned.

"No I didn't. I just gave you love taps. Mel thought it might be an incentive to you. Good night."

The men got into their car and drove off. Seth lay holding his knee and whining until the pain lessened a little. He dragged himself up and into his car. Thank goodness no one had come along. He had to get the money.

A few days later Seth received a phone call at the office from his Dad.

"Dad, I asked you not to call me here."

"First time and it's very important.

"Better be."

"Remember I told you that your Mom felt a lot more pain than she lets on?"

"Yes."

"Well, it's gotten much worse. They can't control it at home, and they want to put her in the hospital or a hospice where they can administer and monitor a higher dose of painkillers. The doctor says she hasn't got much longer."

"Sounds like you should do what they say." He tried not to feel pleased at this news.

"She's scared. She doesn't want to go. Feels she won't last a week in the hospital."

"What can I do?"

"A lot. Come over tonight and I'll tell you."

Seth went. After he talked with his mother, he settled with his father in the living room with their beers.

"What's this about?" Seth asked.

"Your mother and I want to go together."

"Go where?"

"Go? Go? Go. Die, you dummy."

"What?"

"Your mother wants to end her pain. If your mother dies, I don't want to live without her. We need your help."

"How?" Seth asked defensively.

"Help us die together."

"You want to die and want me to help you? That's crazy. That's murder. I'll go to prison," Seth sputtered.

"No, you won't. We'll make it look like suicide. I've written a suicide note. We tried it once but I screwed it up. We need you to see we get the right dose and stay until we're gone. Last time I didn't give us enough medicine and we woke up. You'll get the money you're so worried about. Think about that."

Seth sucked on his beer bottle. The idea offended what remained of his Christian inclinations, but those emotions clashed against the fear of a beating or worse by Mel and his gang. Besides, the old folks wanted him to do it.

"You still got any whiskey around?"

"Yes, we hardly touched that bottle of Irish whiskey you gave us a couple of Christmases ago. It's in the counter under the dinnerware drawer."

Seth went into the kitchen, found the bottle, and poured himself about three ounces. He drank part of it down and then put some water and more whiskey into the glass. It warmed his stomach. He thought about the proposal. Seth didn't have many scruples to overcome, and he quickly accomplished that chore. He walked back into the living room and sat down opposite his Dad. "What exactly do you want me to do?"

"Simple. We've saved up medicine over time. We've got enough for three or four lethal doses. At least according to the Physicians' Desk Reference."

"But murder?" Seth still struggled with what little remained of his conscience.

"It's not murder. You'll help us. It's an act of mercy. Blessed are the merciful."

"You're sure?"

"Yes, we've talked and prayed over this a long time. Help us. You're the only one who can do it," he pleaded.

"Let me talk to Mom alone."

Thirty minutes later Seth left his mom's bedside convinced that she felt excruciating pain when not medicated. She wanted relief, permanent relief.

"What do you want me to do?" Seth asked John.

"Come into the kitchen."

On the kitchen counter sat two mounds of white powder and two glasses.

"I ground up all the remaining pills we had. Here's the result."

"And?"

"Put one mound of the powder in each glass, mix it up good, put a straw in one glass, and give it to Mom. I'll drink mine when she's finished hers. Then wait until we've passed out and leave. Our troubles, and yours, will end."

Seth did as his father told him and took one glass to his mother. He asked again, "Are you sure, Mom?" as he handed her the glass.

"We've prayed. This is what I want to do. Help me."

Seth held the glass while his mother emptied it through the straw. The old couple then sat holding hands and watching the TV with the sound turned off.

"Thanks, Son," she said as she closed her eyes. Shortly, she seemed to go to sleep. Her breathing slowed.

"It's working," John said. He drank his glass. Seth sat and watched while his mother's breathing grew shallower and shallower then seemed to cease. Seth looked at his dad. He slumped in the chair with his head bent forward on his chest. Seth walked over to one then the other. He could see no breathing. In a mixed state of shock, horror, and relief, he finished his whiskey, turned and moved quickly out the door, and jumped in his car. As he drove away he called Mel on his cell phone.

As Seth called, John slowly raised his head, reached out a feeble hand, and punched the 911 preset button.

"Man," the EMS attendant said, "we made it just in time for the old lady. We got her pumped out. She'll do OK once she gets to the hospital."

"What about the old guy?" Detective Garza asked.

"He responded pretty quickly. When we got him pumped out he seemed alert, but he's weak. He's over eighty you know. You can talk to him at the hospital too. He'll tell you why we called you."

"Hey, Garza. What's the story on the attempted suicides you caught last night?" Maloney called out.

"No suicide, attempted murder. We picked up the son at his home. It looks like he got in deep to a Mafia loan guy and figured this as his chance to get the mob off his back."

"How did you find that out?"

"The old man told us."

"The guy tried to kill his parents? What a scumbag! Got a good case?"

"Lock cinch. The perp's wife confirmed he'd pestered the old folks for money. Then, according to the old man, he came over last night and threatened them if they didn't promise to give him $200,000. They refused. He knocked out the old man and then it appears that he forced medicine down his mother's throat. Apparently he did the same to his dad."

"Will they stand up in court? Two old people testifying, the defense lawyer will get them all twisted up."

"No way. His fingerprints are all over the glasses. Then there's the bruising on the mother's throat. The old man has a nasty cut on his head."

"How did the old guy survive?"

"The woman's stomach contained lots of drugs, but the geezer had very little. Looks like the guy screwed up. Just like we solve most cases, criminal stupidity. Anyway the son's on the way to the slammer. Maybe his loan guy will catch up with him there."

John slid his walker ahead of him as he approached Mary's bed in the recovery area. "You OK?" he asked as he took her hand.

"Yep, except for the cancer."

"You have always had a weird sense of humor. Guess that's one of the reasons I put up with you so long."

"Well, at least you had a reason," Mary said.

John leaned over and whispered into her ear. "Sorry I squeezed your neck so tight."

"You had to leave a bruise, and I gave you a pretty good whack with that ash tray."

"Just a love tap. Didn't mean to give you so much medicine. That came close."

"Worth the risk."

"Well, I guess that we got rid of our biggest fear. No old folks home for us. Beat him to the punch."

"Yup," she said, squeezing his hand. "We're still a good team."

Momma's Rally

He loved football, until he broke his neck. Now he couldn't stand it. He could not stand the fact that the so-called premier educational institution in the state wasted all that time and money on holding a gathering, a rally, for a football game. It reminded him too intensely of the time, money, and life he had wasted on football.

When it happened, everyone felt sorry. The school paid for most of the hospitalization and the rehab. However, none of them lay in the hospital bed for six months with a "crown" holding their head steady with screws in their skull. Nor did they endure the months of grinding, boring, punishing rehab work, as well as the pulverizing, immobilizing depression. He worked hard, and in due course he started moving his fingers and toes. Eventually he could move enough to get into a mechanical wheelchair. They kept calling him lucky.

One year later he restarted classes. Right after the injury some of his freshman teammates and the linebacker coach used to come to see him. In a few months, when the novelty wore off, that stopped. His girlfriend, or former girlfriend, came only twice. She told his best buddy to tell him that hospitals depressed her, so she wouldn't come anymore. She said to call her when he got out. Fat chance. He was left alone with his headaches and his thoughts. Even the hospital chaplain turned into a pain in the ass. Not that he went to church often once he left Big Spring to go to the university. Only Momma's regular visits kept him motivated. Even his dad did not come much.

Before it happened, before he ever went to the university, playing football and hunting summed up his activities in Big Spring. He held a few easy jobs because they knew him as a football hero, but most of the time he worked out or hung out. His high school team won the district championship, but he was the only one on the team to get a scholarship offer from a big-time school. Everyone called this great. Not how it turned out.

He got his injury in a simple play, in only the second scrimmage, when he wanted to impress the coaches. He wanted them to see that the country boys from the small school could play with the big boys. He heard the count, saw the snap of the ball, the handoff, and the all conference fullback heading to the hole in front of him. He drove off his right leg from his crouch position to put a hit on the guy and drive him back. But he'd misjudged the fullback; he was a 250-pounder headed for the pros, not one of the 180-pound backs from Killeen or Woodville he used to knock on their butts. The impact caught his head at an angle, drove it back, and cracked three cervical vertebrae. The scrimmage stopped. Eventually he went off in an ambulance to the emergency room. The next thing he knew, he woke up three days later with the metal halo on, unable to move. He screamed and then cried for Momma, who'd sat in the hall, waiting.

After he got out of the hospital and began rehab, he had nothing to do with football, the team, or his old teammates. He stayed too busy trying to find out who, and what, he was. He tried to do school work, make new friends, rehab, and fight off the depression the therapist called normal. The player who injured him never showed up. Part of the game, the fullback told someone.

Only Momma kept up her visits and though at times he didn't want to see her, he had to admit that he liked her coming. He tried to continue school because she wanted him to graduate. However, school only covered up the increasing bitterness in his heart against the money-making system that had put him in the wheelchair and abandoned him. With that impassioned mindset, he read in the college paper about the game and the big rally this weekend. He thought that he'd make an appearance.

The morning of the rally, he motored his chair over to the closet where the people who moved him had dumped all his stuff from the athletic dorm over a year ago. He had a hard time sorting through things with the mechanical device that helped his arm move, but he found what he wanted. His AK-47 assault rifle that he bought his senior year in high school, just in case. He bought it easily in Dallas. He told the guy he bought it from he just wanted to do some shooting in Montana. The weapon weighed 11.31 pounds with a loaded 30 round magazine. He loaded only ten rounds so he could handle it easier. He'd rather take one of his hunting rifles, but knew he couldn't hold it steady.

Two hours before the rally's start at the stage near the main fountain, he struggled into his letterman's jacket, courtesy of the boosters club, which did not contribute to his medical bills, and set out for the library. Because of his wheelchair and the fact that the library staff knew him, he didn't have any trouble getting around the metal detectors. The jacket helped, too. The AK-47 lay under his blanket. Good thing it had a folding stock. He rolled into the elevator and punched ten. Getting off, he maneuvered to a little-used research cubicle overlooking the speaking area. He pushed to the window looking down on the fountain, and struggled to lift it a few inches. He found the binoculars he had left there the day before. He had a good view. Opening his pack, he took a double dose of his meds with bottled water. He hoped they'd end the pounding in his head. He started his wait.

He began thinking about his "project." According to the school paper, the university president, the athletic director, and the football coach all planned to speak. Beat State, they'd say. I haven't learned much since I got here, he thought, but you'd think the president would have a lot more to do than lead cheers. At least the athletic director knows he's milking the system. And the coach makes over $1,000,000 a year (daddy was lucky to make $30,000 in a real good year) getting young men to commit legalized assault and battery all week and on the weekend.

I'm an extreme example, but not one man finishes football in college without some physical injury. Well, maybe I'll get all three if I can hold this thing steady. Too bad I can't hold and sight it. However, with this baby I can point in the general direction, squeeze, and get somebody. After the cheerleaders whip up a little frenzy and the band starts the old fight song, the dignitaries will appear front and center. Only a little while now. His body shook.

When he came to the university, he promised Momma he'd make a name for himself. His day had arrived.

The music started. He manhandled the gun on to the window ledge and aimed it at the speaker's stand. As the band played, he looked down as an older woman walked up to the podium with papers in her hand. She looked like Momma. The same chunky build, short gray hair, and height as Momma. His head shook as a migraine flashed from the base of his skull to his eyes.

His eyes filled with water. What's Momma doing here? He put the weapon down and wiped his eyes. When he looked down again the woman still fussed with the papers. It was Momma. She had on her favorite "go to meeting" blue dress. He picked up his binoculars.

Through still damp eyes he saw her walking off the stage. His mind ached and spun. Bolts of pain boomeranged in his skull. He wanted Momma to feel proud of him, but he didn't want her here. The fight song reached a crescendo and caused him more stabs of pain. He held his head in his hands and saw Momma hugging him before Daddy drove him down to early practice.

Then he heard Momma say sharply, "No boy, stop whatever you're doing this second. Get in here—now! What do you think you're up to?"

His head snapped up as it had when, as a small boy into mischief, he heard her voice. His mind started clearing. He looked around, trying to figure out where he was.

Still dazed, he put the weapon under his blanket, spun his chair, and rolled toward the elevator. "Coming, Momma."

On the stage, Mary Wilson, the president's longtime, grey-haired secretary, walked over to the president and told him she had arranged his speech on the podium and took her seat.

Heirloom

Hannah stormed into her office, snarled a greeting at her P.A., and threw her briefcase on to her visitor's chair. Hannah did not take losing anything kindly, particularly a negotiation to Joe Miller, her personal nemesis. Especially when her clients were in the right as, of course, they always were.

"Goddamn Miller. He wouldn't know a good settlement if it bit him in the ass," she fumed.

Fidalia, the P.A., let her fulminate. From years of experience she knew this as the best course of action. When she heard the third drawer slam shut, she recognized her cue to ease into Hannah's office.

"Didn't settle the case, huh?"

"Don't be a smart ass, Fidalia." The five-foot-seven slender trial attorney spit out. "He just aggravates the hell out of me. Arrogant male. Whaddaya got?"

"Your uncle Abe called. Sounded important. Something about a bracelet. Wants you to call him."

The words Uncle Abe and bracelet in the same sentence slowed Hannah down. "OK, get him for me."

Hannah sat down in her desk chair and swiveled it until she looked east out the window towards a cityscape, and her mind's eye transformed the view into an old European city.

That damn bracelet, she thought. Why wouldn't the old people let it go?

The buzzer sounded and she picked up the phone. "Hello, Uncle Abe. What's new?"

Hannah listened while her octogenarian uncle explained in his accented voice that he had received advice from their friends in Europe that they had another lead to the location of the family heirloom. Abe ended the message with a request, no, an order, that she come to his house that night to meet with him and her two equally ancient aunts, the last survivors of the family from the old country of those who had escaped the Holocaust. The others had died from age and suffering. Hannah's parents had been killed in an automobile accident in Florida ten years ago.

Even though all the other tips had led to futile quests, the old people held strong emotions about the bracelet. The Nazis had taken it from the matriarch of the family when they were arrested in Berlin in the late thirties. The last symbol of a once proud, brilliant family, they wanted the symbol, their Holy Grail, back.

Now the old folks thought they had found it again. Hannah knew little about the people that the relatives had contact with in Europe. She didn't know if she trusted them. They claimed a mission to help survivors recover property confiscated by the Nazis. They were not a charity, however, as they requested ten percent of the value of the items recovered for expenses. Not an unreasonable fee, and being a private group, they could sometimes use means that might not be acceptable to others.

Abe told Hannah, "The group contacted us. They say they have reliable information that a Dutchman tried to sell the bracelet to one of their contacts, a jeweler in Amsterdam. They could set up a meeting with the seller in Amsterdam if the family wanted to deal directly. In addition they'd supply support."

Hannah knew that in the end she'd agree with the old people to go and try to recover the bracelet. Her brother was too busy with his medical practice and they were too frail. Furthermore, years of listening to the stories of her relatives and their friends about events in Europe in the thirties and forties made her feel guilty for not being there to help even though she had not been born yet. She had to make this trip for her family.

Fedalia booked Hannah into the Krasnapolsky Hotel in Amsterdam on short notice. She had stayed there before on business, so that eased the way. The KLM flight had been uneventful as was the train ride to the center of town. Being known at the hotel gave her a secure feeling.

Once in the hotel, Hannah bathed and napped to be alert for the evening the friends had arranged for her. The only disturbance was a phone call from her Uncle's friends, followed by the arrival of some flowers, an envelope, and a box of chocolates.

She sat down on the bed to absorb the information she received in the note and to examine the contents of the box. When the time approached to leave the hotel, she dressed in her lawyer's uniform, a dark blue trouser suit and a white silk blouse. She wore no jewelry and little make up. Her black hair was cut short. Just the appearance a forty-two year old lawyer needed for the most important negotiation of her life, even bigger than the Texcal merger. That was only business, this was more significant.

The hotel's location on Dam Square was walking distance to the Rembrandtsplein, where she was to meet a man named Ulrik. Hannah left the hotel in plenty of time to arrive before eight o'clock.

Still light out as she briskly strode across the canal bridge. She might have found the walk along the canal pleasant under different circumstances, but Hannah's trepidation grew with each step. She had no idea of the personality of the man she was to meet.

The family had decided that they'd pay a finder's fee only, no blood money. If the man didn't accept their proposal, they told her they would find other means to retrieve the bracelet. She wasn't sure she liked the sound of that, but she decided to leave the debate over the justice of using unjust means to right a wrong to the rabbis, priests, to other ethicists.

Hannah patted her purse and felt the presence of the small Beretta pistol and cell phone that had been delivered to her room with the flowers. The Beretta was loaded, and she thought she remembered how to use it from the training she received as an assistant district attorney many years ago. Hannah paid little attention to the tourists and local people starting to fill the streets.

Arriving at the Café Reynders, she failed to see a single male at any of the tables. Taking a seat at an outdoor table, she ordered coffee. She thought the crowd was thin for the entertainment district, but she reasoned it was still early in the evening. Hannah's gaze swept the sidewalks. Finally, she spotted a man half a block away, walking quicker than the others. Most people strolled and stopped to look at the pictures that advertised the district's late night, mostly female, entertainment.

The man drew closer. As he neared, she guessed his height at about five-foot-ten. He had a solid frame and his receding hair was cut close and graying at the temples.

Still closer, Hannah saw dark eyes, an undistinguished nose, and thin lips. A small scar punctuated the left side of the upper lip. He was dressed in a black leather jacket, blue jeans, and a work shirt open at the collar. Hannah put his age at late fifties or early sixties.

Striding directly to Hannah's table, he offered, "I am Ulrik." He offered his hand. His voice was low and guttural, his words clipped and precise. She recognized immediately that English was not his native tongue.

She took his firm handshake. His hand felt like it was used for carpentry or other manual labor.

"You are Hannah?"

"Right."

"You are interested in purchasing a bracelet I have?"

"Maybe, let's talk."

"How did you hear about me?" he asked.

"The jeweler you took the bracelet to for appraisal contacted me about it."

"You came all the way from the States to buy?"

"No, I'm in the jewelry business," Hannah lied. "I come here two or three times a year to buy diamonds."

"Let's go inside to discuss business," Ulrik said. He led the way into the café and went to small table in the rear area of the bar. Hannah followed.

"Would you like a drink?" he asked.

"Another black coffee please."

So far things had proceeded correctly and cordially.

Ulrik signaled the waitress. "A black coffee and a double cognac."

"I'm selling this bracelet for family," Ulrik started. "The jeweler's appraisal is not good, too little. I need twice amount so I will sell privately. I want price, in cash, in guilders."

"You're ahead of yourself, Ulrik. Let's be sure what we're talking about." Hannah produced a five-by-seven black and white picture of a bracelet. The picture, dark and old, dimly showed a braided rope bracelet made of alternate shaded colored strands, possibly gold and silver. Instead of one circle it looked as if it could wind around a wrist two or three times. In the center sat a larger jewel that could be a diamond. Other jewels were evenly spaced along the rope.

"Yes, that looks like my bracelet," Ulrik said. "If you talked to the jeweler you know."

"I spoke to him briefly. All he said was that you had a bracelet I might be interested in buying. Where did you get it?"

"It has been my family's since 1918. One of my ancestors was a Dutch ship captain. He performed special services for Russian Royal family during Revolution. It was given him as a reward for those services."

Nonsense, thought Hannah.

"Why hasn't your family sold it before? To be blunt, you don't seem rich."

"The bracelet was lost in flood when the Allies bombed dams in war. We found it when digging to expand house."

Unlikely, thought Hannah. "Do you have any papers or provenance to support your ownership?" she asked.

"No, you take as is."

The waitress appeared with cognac and coffee. They both sipped their drinks as she moved away.

Hannah put down her cup. She looked Ulrik in the eye and said firmly, "Your story is bogus. If the bracelet you have is the one in the picture, it was taken from my grandmother when she was arrested in her home in Berlin in 1942."

"Not true. The war over for fifty-five years. All stolen Nazis things have been returned or destroyed." He rose to leave.

"Sit down," she commanded in the firmest lawyer's tone she could muster, just like the one she used to talk to Miller.

"Let me tell you a story. Then, maybe, we can make a deal."

Ulrik hesitated, glared, but sat back down.

"When my grandmother and her family were arrested in Berlin it was a very nice and polite police procedure. The officer in charge,

Otto Skorez, was a friend of the family in better days. Grandmother was scared. He told her she would just be processed at the police station and then probably could come home. She didn't believe him, but thinking of him as a friend of the family, she gave him her jewels and some money and asked him to give them to her sister. She hoped it would help her sister escape. Skorez said he would and that all would be well when she came back from the police station. She never came back. The jewelry and money never got to her sister, my great aunt.

"That bracelet, the one you have, was given to my great, great grandfather by Czar Nicholas II of Russia. It carries a special blessing in the Cyrillic alphabet incorporated in the design. If you don't know the alphabet or don't know where to look for it, you won't see it. The jeweler saw it. That's why he called me."

"I've never been to Berlin. Why is this your bracelet?"

"Because your grandfather served in the Nazi Dutch Corps during World War II."

"A lie. He was in the underground. He a Dutch hero."

"Listen Ulrik. Cut the crap. The Russians in Berlin captured Skorez. Before his capture, he gave the bracelet and money to his aide, your grandfather, to give to Skorez's wife. Your grandfather still had his Dutch papers. He figured he could claim association with the underground. He was captured and brought to Berlin. His plan worked. The Russians let him go. However, he never delivered the bracelet. Apparently theft ran in the unit."

"Why not arrest Skorez?" Ulrik scoffed.

"Skorez died in a Russian prison camp and no one really cared what happened to the items stolen by the Nazis until recently. Everyone pretended this type of theft didn't happen. Now we hear descriptions of stolen paintings, jewelry and the like from all over the world."

"I know nothing of this."

"Yes, you do. A man fitting your description brought this bracelet to the antique shop of Smit van Oss on Spiegel Straat here in Amsterdam for an appraisal. The appraisal was given orally. When he was asked to leave the bracelet so that a written appraisal could be prepared, the man, you, refused and left the store in a hurry. Fortunately for us the appraiser is a member of the United Nation sponsored European jewelers group that catalogs jewelry reported stolen by the Nazis. He gave a description of the bracelet to the registry in London and they identified it."

So far the information Hannah had been supplied with seem to be hitting the mark.

Ulrik began clenching and unclenching his right hand as Hannah continued.

"The registry had a report of the theft by Skorez from prison camp survivors. The Germans kept very thorough records. German Army files show Skorez's last assignment in Berlin and a roster of his unit. Your grandfather was listed as his aide with responsibilities for Dutch matters."

Ulrik said boldly, "So what? If is true, it would have been claimed long ago."

"Maybe in a better world. If the Swiss wouldn't give up their gold until world wide pressure was put on them, what chance does one dead person's family have? The theft of one bracelet was lost in the search for millions of dollars worth of stolen property. That is, until you appeared with the bracelet."

"You're trying to steal bracelet from me," Ulrik said dropping his voice to a harsh whisper. "Why don't I throw you in canal?"

"Your greed stops you." The two stared intently at each other with deep distaste in their eyes. "Greed and the fact that you're not that dumb."

Ulrik grunted.

"Listen to my proposition," Hannah commanded.

"I'll listen, but I need good money." Ulrik settled in his chair and tossed down the rest of his cognac.

Hannah leaned forward to emphasize her words. "I'll give you a finder's fee of ten thousand dollars for the bracelet. That's it. Oh yes, and no questions asked and no report to authorities."

"Kack. You're a thief. It's worth ten times that. I'll get my price from someone. Damn authorities no worry me, but you should have worry walking by the canals." He roughly shoved back his chair and started out.

"Sit down," Hannah ordered. "There's more."

"A lot more is needed." Ulrik sat but only on the front of his chair.

"You have a son named Hanspeter, don't you Ulrik?"

"How do you know? He has nothing to do with this."

"How I know is not important. I want you to talk to someone." Hannah pulled out the cell phone that had come with the Beretta, pushed a preset number, and handed the phone to Ulrik.

"Hello, Hello. Who is this? Maria? It's me, Ulrik."

He wondered how Hannah had his number. "Ulrik, thank God. Where are you? I'm scared."

"What's wrong?"

"It's Hanspeter. On his way home from his piano lesson last night he was stopped and roughed up by a couple of men."

"My God. How is he?"

"He is frightened but OK."

"Who did it?"

"We have no idea. He really didn't see them well."

"What did the police say?"

"Nothing. We didn't call them."

"For Christ sakes, why not?"

"Because he wasn't badly hurt and he couldn't identify them. But, mostly because of what they said. That's what really scares me."

"What?"

"They called him a Nazi and a thief and said you were too. They said the next time it would be his fingers. Ulrik, what's going on?"

"I'll be home as soon as I can. Don't talk to anyone. Goodbye. "

He tossed the phone at Hannah. It bounced off her arm and on to the table. She calmly picked it up and put it in her purse, letting her hand linger near the pistol.

"Who are you, what do you want?" he hissed.

"I'm the person who wants her family's stolen heirloom back, and I don't want to wait while a bunch of courts and commissions sort through a lot of lies and denials. I'm also a person with friends who feel the same way about Nazi thefts and are interested in righting a few wrongs in the world. We know your most precious possession is not the bracelet, but your son and his musical talent. He's been offered a place in the Amsterdam Music Conservatory," Hannah said the words that she had read in the letter she received at the hotel.

"You bitch. You threatened hands?"

"No. I threatened nothing. I think what your son's visitors might have said was something about the next time, his hands. I'm proposing there be no next time. It's up to you."

"What do you want?"

"Just what I said. I'll trade your precious possession for my family's heirloom. On top of that I'll pay you $10,000, tell the registry that the piece has been found, and assure you that these men will not visit Hanspeter again."

"*Evil* woman," Ulrik spit.

"Excuse me if I laugh. Evil! You can talk evil with the relatives of people taken from their homes for no reason and never seen again. We're trying to right a wrong here."

Ulrik squeezed his cognac glass until Hannah thought it would shatter.

"Hanspeter knows nothing. He is completely innocent."

"As was my grandmother," Hannah said her blood pressure rising. Sweat began to emerge on the back of her neck. Hannah continued more calmly. "I'll give you forty-eight hours to accept my offer. If you accept, take the bracelet to the same jeweler who appraised it for you. He will expect you. He'll examine it and if it is what we think it is, he'll give you ten thousand dollars in guilders. If you don't show up, you might want to get back the deposit you put on the apartment for Hanspeter while he studies at the conservatory. You can use it for hand surgery." She delivered the words with a zeal she really didn't feel.

Ulrik looked into Hannah's eyes and saw a burning intensity. He began to believe. Ulrik threw back his chair.

"I'll think about it," he said angrily as he strode toward the door almost knocking over an incoming customer.

As he went out the door, a sigh escaped Hannah's lips. Tension oozed from her body. She shuddered. Give me Miller anytime, she thought and then signaled for a cognac. He'll show up at the jewelers, she thought, trying to reassure herself, then decided it was best to take a taxi back to the hotel.

A Special Job

Peter waited nervously on the street corner. He'd never met Karl, only answered an ad in a counter-culture newspaper. Peter spotted a white male walking aggressively in his direction. The man looked about six feet tall, slender built, probably weighing around 175 to 180. His receding red hair was close cut and graying at the temples. As the man walked up to him, Peter could see very dark eyes and a flat nose and thin lips. A small strawberry birthmark was on the left end of his upper lip.

Neatly dressed in a blue sport coat, blue button-down shirt, opened at the collar, and khaki slacks, he looked like he'd arrived right from an Ivy League campus or a Land's End catalog, or both. More respectable than Peter had anticipated.

Peter put the man's age somewhere in the late fifties or early sixties. Again different than he had imagined, older. I hope he's right for the job, Peter thought.

The man's handshake felt firm, but not objectionably so. His hand had the callous one gets from manual labor.

He spoke in a low and clear voice. He used clipped and precise words, as if his native tongue was something other than English.

"I am Karl", he said. "You are Peter?'

"Yes."

"About your 'special job', you agree to my terms?"

"Yes, I have to. They're driving me nuts. Here's half your money. I'll send the rest when the job's done."

"Agreed."

"Here's my address. You'll find them playing in the backyard at six p.m. Sunday. I'll distract the rest in the upstairs TV room. And I don't want to see them again."

"You won't. One question."

"What?'

"Why did you give your kids rabbits for Easter in the first place?"

Reluctant Dane

A patch on the eye. Some disguise for a spy. Soren had to turn his head to see the Tuborg beer and aquavit the waiter had set on the edge his table. He sat at the Divan 1 Restaurant in Tivoli Garden. The doctor told him he'd have to wear the eye patch a short time after the cataract operation.

He found it hard enough to go about without being noticed. Spies were supposed to blend into the background. Not that he was a spy, of course. He was just an artist who helped Israeli intelligence, the Mossad. He passed tidbits he picked up on the diplomatic cocktail circuit from time to time. Official Israeli contact by the Danes was carried on through the embassy. Unofficially, a second level allowed the Mossad to track the many immigrants from various Arab countries in Africa and the Middle East living in Copenhagen.

Most were true refugees escaping the oppression of the regimes in Libya, Iraq, Iran, or Syria, but they provided good cover for terrorists. Denmark's liberal entrance policies made keeping out suspects very difficult. The terrorists did not operate in Denmark, but they found it a good base to operate from for all of Europe.

Mossad took advantage of Danish cooperation by identifying potential terrorists. But they took no action in Denmark, waiting until the suspects moved elsewhere to conduct an operation.

Soren's recruitment as a unofficial katsis by the Mossad was strange. He was not Jewish, as were almost all Israeli agents. Fifteen years ago he was a young talented Danish filmmaker. Now he was a painter. Then he had made a movie that was both a critical and commercial success about the Danes saving almost all Jews in Denmark from the Nazis in World War II. When the Nazi occupiers ordered a round up of Jews, word was passed to the Danish underground. Overnight, the Danish people had smuggled the majority of Danish Jews by boat to neutral Sweden.

As a result of the movie, Soren received a number of awards from, among others, the Israeli film industry and the Israeli government. He became friends with members of the Israeli embassy staff. Then one evening, one of the staff asked him to pass on to an Israeli friend anything he thought interesting. He agreed. Whether he knew it or not, he had been recruited.

The success of his movie also ensured that he had the money to devote full time to his first love, painting. No more crass grubbing for money in the film world. At least not for a while.

On January 13, 1991, he received a phone call. His Israeli friend asked him to be at the Divan 1 Restaurant in Tivoli at two p.m. tomorrow.

"Wear a blue hat and have a copy of one of the local newspapers, the *Politiken*. Someone will meet you and give you information."

"Why can't somebody from the embassy go?" Soren asked

"Too obvious."

"Can't I meet him in secret?"

"Too obvious. It must look like a casual meeting."

"Plau. I'll be there," Soren said reluctantly.

A few days before the phone call, the United States government, on behalf of a consortium, announced that if the Iraqis did not withdraw from Kuwait, that on January 15,1999 at five p.m. the consortium would attack Iraq.

Dumb Americans, he thought when he had read about it. Did they mean five p.m. Washington time, European time, or Iraqi time? A small thing, but lesser things had caused bloodshed that should not have happened. Oh well, it had no immediate effect on him. That changed.

As a result of the announcement of the planned attack, U.S. installations around the world were put on alert regarding possible terrorist attacks. Because such terrorist attacks might be launched against American business overseas, as well as against government and military facilities, the embassies were told to alert and brief U.S. businesses.

Each U.S. company in Denmark, more than one hundred of them, was asked to send a representative to a security briefing session in the embassy in Copenhagen at ten a.m. on January 14th, the day before the deadline.

When the representatives arrived at the Embassy, they each went through security before they entered the building. As a result, certain interested Arabs noted that about one hundred American businessmen would be standing outside the embassy a little before ten a.m. on January 14th waiting to be searched one by one before they could enter the embassy.

On January 12th, three Arabs sat in a room at the Sheraton hotel. They had met before but not often. A heated discussion ensued.

"We know that the Americans plan to attack. We should strike first. We should not let this opportunity pass," Fuad said heatedly.

"No," said Moussa, the PLO representative. "We met here only to gather information. We're not an action group. Besides, I have no action directive from my headquarters. Saddam's action will not help the Palestinian people. A terrorist act here and now does not help the people."

Khalid, who had loose connections with the Libyan government, also objected to action. He stayed silent. He liked living in Copenhagen more than Tripoli, Libya. He liked the few hundred extra dollars a month he picked up from the Libyan government. He only had to pass on information he heard from the Danish, U.S., and other government officials who ate at the upscale restaurant where he worked as the maitre'd. He wanted no part of murder.

Their cowardice made Fuad furious. After an hour of arguing, smoking, and drinking non-Muslim whiskey, he stood up and said that it fell to him to act as the sword of Allah. He stormed out of the room.

Moussa said to Khalid, "I hope that is just the whiskey talking."

"I do, too," replied Khalid.

The two men then finished the Scotch while discussing the prospect of the Danish soccer teams in the European cup starting next week. They agreed the Danes would not last long. Moussa paid the room charges as they left.

Worry plagued the PLO man. He wanted to gather information only. An attack presented a problem. No murders would get by the avengers. It didn't matter who got hurt as long as they delivered a lesson. The killing continued back and forth until someone decided to stop. "I don't want it to start here," Moussa thought. He found a public phone and placed a call to a secure number at the Israeli embassy.

"This is Hans Christian," he said when someone answered the phone. "Is my plane ticket ready?"

"Let me check. Yes, you can pick up your tickets for the Canary Islands after ten tomorrow."

At ten in the morning the next day Moussa sauntered along the crowded walks of Tivoli Garden. As he passed the Divan 1 Restaurant he saw a man sitting alone, wearing an eye patch, a blue hat, and reading a copy of the the *Politiken*. Moussa sat on one of the benches across from the restaurant and pretended to read his paper. He checked out the other patrons at the Divan and the restaurants on either side of it as well as the people walking by. After ten minutes, he had seen nothing that caused him concern. He strode over to Soren's table and sat down.

"Tell your friends that someone may attack the American embassy tomorrow."

"Why not tell the Americans?"

"I did but they have gotten a lot of calls. I didn't identify myself so they think it's from another crank."

"Why tell anyone?"

"I don't want it to succeed."

"How will it happen?"

"I don't know. A man named Fuad said he'd act alone so we have no informant. The Israelis have a dossier on him. They can stop him. That's all know. You're warned." Moussa rose and maneuvered his way through the tables and back into the crowd.

Soren passed the information to his contact at the Israeli Embassy. Two agents went to Fuad's apartment. No response to a door rap. They let themselves in and found no indication that anyone had stayed there last evening. Visits to his known haunts turned up no information about his whereabouts.

The local control made a hurried secure call to Paris. He requested an agent authorized to perform a wet job, a killer. They needed the assassin by tomorrow morning. Paris said that they'd do what they could but they had heavy rain and fog in Paris. This had delayed flights the past few mornings.

"*Godaften*," Soren said when he answered a late evening call.

"We need your help again," declared the familiar voice. "We can't locate the man. Help arrives sometime tomorrow, but we need you 'til then."

Soren sputtered his objections but then followed his caller's direction to call back from a public phone. Soren got his instructions.

At nine the morning of January 15, 1991, Soren sat in a dark blue BMW with Danish diplomatic license plates. Wearing a chauffeur's cap, he sat in a parallel parking slot reserved for diplomats' cars outside the United States embassy. His passenger had entered the embassy through the diplomatic entrance. He called his control on the radio. "I'm here. When will the other fellow join me?"

"His plane was delayed. We'll rush him over when he lands. If anything unusual happens, call me. I'll tell the others down the street and they will help you."

"They'd better. I've no weapon and couldn't use it if I did."

"Don't worry," control said. He wasn't as confident as he sounded.

By nine forty-five a crowd of thirty-five to fifty people had gathered outside the embassy and waited for the slow processing and body searches inside the embassy.

Soren could see two apparent agents twenty or thirty yards in front of him. He thought that they were a long way away. He also saw a man with a red hat and a man with a yellow jacket on the outside in the crowd at the door. They had remained on the outside of the crowd since he got in place. The Israeli agents made no attempt to enter the building, but their stalling appeared obvious to anyone watching them.

The busy traffic moved on the wide street in two generous lanes for cars in either direction. Outside lanes remained open for the omnipresent Danish bicyclists.

Suddenly something stirred at the front door. Soren stiffened. Four uniform guards and two men in civilian suits approached the two Israelis on the edge of the crowd. The guards and others quickly patted them down and quickly and efficiently ushered the Israelis into the embassy. Soren remained alone out in front. He had lost some of his help.

He looked around to see if anyone was approaching his car. As he turned his head back to the front, a bicycle, ridden by a man in a black jacket and black crash helmet, jumped the curb and started to the crowd in front of the embassy. Unfortunately for the cyclist, he had to swerve to avoid a woman with a baby carriage. He skidded. Attention focused on him. He swung his right arm up and over his head. His briefcase started an arched flight toward the crowd. Because of his hurried throw, his lack of arm strength, or the weight of the briefcase, the case landed ten yards short of the crowd. People scattered.

The car motor was running for warmth. As Soren saw the briefcase start its parabola toward the people, he jammed down on the accelerator. Jerking the steering wheel to the right, he aimed the car through an opening between two of the large planters, spaced evenly across the front of the plaza where it joined the public sidewalk.

Soren did not know that the planters formed part of the upgraded security system at U.S. embassies around the world. Designers had made the heavily reinforced hunks of concrete specifically to prevent cars from driving into the front of U.S. installations.

Soren's car shot into the opening. The sound of ripping, scraping metal cut through the air. The car almost came to a halt. Then, as if pushed by some hidden hand, it eased through the opening and exploded forward. Dazed by the impact, Soren slammed on the breaks and the car skidded to a halt. The briefcase was under his side of the car. Most of the car rested between the brief case and the embassy entrance.

On January 16 the *Politiken* reported one dead and over thirty injured in an explosion at the embassy. The dead man's mutilation prevented immediate identification, but apparently he worked as a driver for the Danish embassy.

On January 18, 1991, buried in the news of the invasion of Iraq, the U.S. State Department announced the reopening of its hearings on embassy security. One of the items on the agenda was to the placement of security barriers.

That same day, on the third page of the second section of the *Politiken* appeared a two-paragraph story that reported that in the excitement of the bombing, only two blocks from the embassy, a car hit and killed a cyclist. The police did not think the two matters related. The cyclist had no papers on him and remained unidentified. The police believed him southern European or Middle Eastern.

Operation Eternal Rest

Larry sat in the deck chair sipping his beer and watching his seven-year-old son, Nick, toss his rubber football as far into the sky as he could and then rush over to catch it. He caught the ball using varied styles, some with the right hand, some with the left, some diving and a few, unsuccessful, behind his back. When he made a tough catch, he fell to the ground and yelled "Touchdown!" Occasionally he'd spike the ball into the ground like he had seen on TV. Nick seemed to have an unlimited store of energy.

"Nick, you can't spike the ball in college. You'll get penalized."

"OK, Dad, I'll just do it in the pros or when it's the winning touchdown in the last seconds against Oklahoma."

Larry smiled. Nick possessed brains and athletic skill, but he'd be average-sized like his mom and dad. The possibilities of college or pro football seemed unlikely, but let him dream. He could get the football bug out of his system in high school like Larry did.

Larry felt a poke on his shoulder. He looked around and saw three-year-old Katy with her toy shovel. Apparently Molly, his wife, had let her out into the fenced backyard.

"Hi, Katy. Come on up," Larry said as he lifted her into his lap. A second and harder blow hit his shoulder.

"What? What?" Larry sputtered.

"Wake up, Marine. We've got work to do," Sgt. Brent said. Larry pushed back his helmet, focused his eyes, and looked at the other exhausted Marines trying to nap against the one remaining wall of the burned-out building. The first sixteen hours of the assault had gone on nonstop.

Fighting their way through narrow streets and alleys while carrying a seventy-pound pack and taking fire from the front, side, and back drained body and soul.

Five days into the operation, they still faced exhaustion. Most of the enemy remained in front of them, but they still battled house-to-house, room-to-room. The wall they sheltered behind, probably part of someone's home at one time, now made up just another ruin of the war in Fallujah. Despite the fact that heavy bombardment leveled most of the city, there still had to be boots on the ground, slogging away.

Snipers in the ruins ahead held up Larry's group's advance towards a mosque which intelligence had labeled a terrorist control center. They were to eliminate it.

Achmed had only served a short time in the Iraqi army. The government drafted him and other unemployed Iraqi young men to build up the army in anticipation of an invasion. As a good Sunni, he wanted to defend his country, but he didn't care for army life. However, he was grateful for the pay. His father had died a few years ago when they could not get medicine in his village. He had lost several uncles and cousins in the eight-year war with Iran. Other relatives fell to the enemy during the first invasion.

Hence, Achmed lived in a female-dominated world with food and other support coming from what remained of his extended family. In the army he could send a little money home. He was an intelligent young man. His unit, hastily and poorly trained, was stationed in Baghdad doing manual labor trying to build up its defenses in preparation of an assault on the city. After the Americans invaded in the south, his unit worked faster sandbagging government buildings and other potential targets. It surprised him when, after the message came that the Americans were only days away, he and a few others received instructions to change out of their uniforms, take their weapons, and go home. They were to hide their guns and await further instruction. This puzzled Achmed, but he did as told. He had no desire to get bombed.

Safely back in his village, he returned to his life of unemployment. He visited relatives and friends and played with his little sisters Miriam, seven; Fatima, five; and Shireen, three. He felt sad to see them get thinner and thinner from the shortage of food. His three older brothers, also called to service, were now deployed at various points in Iraq. At times he went to the village square to sit and drink tea with the older men. Normally they'd exclude him because of his youth, but not in these abnormal times. He listened with dismay as refugees from Baghdad told of its occupation by the Americans and the destruction in the city.

One day a man dressed as a mullah visited the village. He called Achmed and two other men to duty. A truck would pick them up in the village center after dawn the day after next. They should not take weapons but take shovels and other tools, as well as food and water for the trip. If stopped, they should say they were going work at a construction site south of Fallujah where the Americans were building a base. Their driver would have papers supporting their story.

Nothing happened during the drive on the dusty road, and the truck delivered them to a small mosque on the south edge of Fallujah. There, others gave them Ak-47s and took them off to learn how to use them effectively. The Russian weapon was cheap and easy to get in quantities, and its thirty-round magazine gave it plenty of fire power. When others saw Achmed's skill as a shooter, they trained him on a bolt-action Finnish made TRG-1 Sniper rifle. It held only ten rounds but when used with a scope, had dead-on accuracy.

Then they assigned Achmed to a group of snipers that had lost fighters in the bombing and shelling. On the fifth day after the Americans had launched their ground attack on Fallujah, Achmed found himself alone on what remained of the roof of a building between the advancing Americans and the Great Mosque. His job, as well as that of the other snipers, was to target American officers, snipers, and any other targets of opportunity.

Achmed had lain prone on the flat roof since before dawn. The previous night the Iraqis saw American troops entering the burned-out house about 300 meters away. Achmed knew his job: to shoot at anyone exposed and keep them pinned down to make them bigger targets for heavier fire. He watched the house from behind a three-foot parapet through a hole where the rainwater drained off the flat roof to barrels below.

Suddenly, someone raised a black flag and waved it from the roof three or four buildings to his left. This signaled to the snipers, scattered across the line of rooftops to Achmed's right and left, to stay alert. Terrorists units planned to attack somewhere along the line of buildings, bringing shooting opportunities for the snipers. Mortar fire started to land near the buildings occupied by the Americans. Achmed looked through the drain hole in the parapet.

"They're trying to bracket us. Let's move out," Sgt. Brent barked. "Get across the street. Larry, cover us in case they've got people on the ground in front of us."

As the first two men prepared to scurry in a low crouch across the street, Larry released the button that limited fire from his M16 A2 to three rounds for one trigger pull. As the men started, he leaned beyond the edge of the wall and sprayed the rubble ahead of him. Achmed, watching through his hole, saw the men hustle across the street and noted the source of the supporting fire. Achmed moved to the left and sighted his weapon as best he could on the shooter's spot in case he came out there again.

As the second two squad members prepared to move across the street, Larry crawled out to fire from a prone position. Achmed adjusted his aim downward and squeezed the trigger; he had over-adjusted, and the shot hit the dirt in front of Larry. Rocks and dirt flew up, lacerating Larry's face. Fortunately Larry had his goggles over his eyes instead of on his helmet like the grunts tended to do, and this saved his eyes. Corp. Jose dragged him back behind the wall. "You OK?" he asked.

"I guess so," Larry replied.

Jose washed away the blood and dirt from the numerous slices and cuts and poured sulfa into some of the deeper ones.

"I spotted him," Jose said.

"Where?"

"On the roof of the brownish building straight ahead. About five yards from the east end of the roof edge, near the water drain.

"I'll get the frigging raghead," Larry said.

"Wait," Jose said. "Let Sam and me get at opposite ends of this wall and draw a bead on him. You get him to pop up again and we'll get him."

Meanwhile, Achmed had moved his position ten yards to the right. He lost his drain hole view, but now they couldn't target him there.

Sam and Jose took their positions at opposite ends of the wall and sighted their weapons where they hoped to see the target.

"OK," Jose signaled Larry, who was to pop out, spray the building to draw fire, and get his butt back behind the wall. However, Larry's adrenaline surged from the facial wounds. Therefore, when he stepped out from the wall, wanting to get the SOB who had shot him, he stopped, aimed, and fired a long burst at the place where Jose indicated the shooter had waited before.

Achmed, yards away from where Larry had aimed, sighted through the scope on Larry and fired. He worked the bolt, sighted again, and fired. When Achmed's head showed, Jose fired.

"Jesus Christ," Larry uttered as a prayer and a curse.

Achmed's first sighted bullet had ripped into Larry's arm. Stunned, Larry turned and Achmed's second shot took him in the neck. Larry's shots had not gone anywhere near Achmed, but Jose's first shot grazed the side of Achmed's head.

"Allah Akbar, God is great," Achmed said as he forgot his training and turned to return fire at the spot where he thought the shot came from. As Achmed turned, Sam sighted and squeezed the trigger of his assault rifle. Three rounds went on their way. The first two missed Achmed, but the third one slammed into his lower jaw and continued upward to tear out the opposite cheek bone.

As Jose worked to staunch the flow of blood from Larry's throat, Larry's mind wandered to thoughts of Molly and Katy cheering Nick as Nick caught a winning touchdown pass for Kelly High School. He prayed for their safety and that Nick would never have to go to war.

Achmed, alone and choking on the blood that drained down his throat, knew death was a short time away. As he lay there praying to Allah, he knew that as a holy warrior, he'd enter Paradise. Therefore, he prayed to Allah not for himself, but for protection for his mother and God's benevolence to allow his sisters Miriam, Fatima, and Shireen to grow up in peace and safety.

Neither race nor religion nor color matters when souls arrive at their final destination. Therefore, Larry and Achmed's ascending souls arrived before the one God at the same cosmic time to start their eternal rest.

Justice

They waited for him in the cemetery behind the church.

Father Sal Rizzano, as the youngest assistant in the parish, stayed to hear the late Saturday confessions while Monsignor Kelly went to his regular Saturday meeting with some of the few of his remaining classmates from the seminary. Hosted in turn by the four grey-haired septuagenarians, they took the opportunity to relax, smoke a good cigar, drink good whiskey—Irish of course—and compare notes on the weird religious practices of their parishioners, many of whom could not separate superstition from faith. God bless them all. Mostly sincere, they meant no damage.

Most of the damage to the Church in current times, the priests had sadly concluded, it inflicted on itself by the return to strict rules adopted by many of the priests to answer to the accusations of abusing children and hiding it. The younger priests hated, to the extent they let themselves hate, those who had brought scorn on the priesthood. They were no modern-day Bing Crosbys, but more pragmatic Barry Fitzgeralds.

While they relaxed, Father Rizzano finished the confessions, then walked the gravel path around the cemetery that backed up to the church property. In this quiet place, he often said the rosary and meditated. Ten times around the path was good exercise. It allowed him plenty of time to finish his prayers, clear his mind, and even give some thoughts to his sermon for the next day. His thoughts also went to the advice he had received from his superiors about exercising cautions in his relationships with the children in the school.

Father Rizzano grew up in a large, warm, demonstrative Italian family, and his superiors in the seminary had noticed his tendency toward "touchy feely." They warned him that in the current climate, someone might misinterpret his well-intentioned touchings and abbraccios (hugs). So he tried to restrain himself, but found it difficult to rein in his Italian outgoing nature. Still, he had never, and, with the Grace of God, would never, touch them in an inappropriate way. Unfortunately, in this era the no-nos included tousling their hair, squeezing their shoulders or arms, or putting his arm around their shoulders.

Furthermore, Father Rizzano didn't know that his predecessor, the young Father Sam Anthony had left on a sudden transfer. No one knew why, but the less charitable in the parish attributed the departure to some unknown thing that happened when he trained the altar boys, a job Father Sal inherited. No facts, only gossip. Msgr. Riley knew of the rumors but felt that denial only added to the problem.

Eight-year-old Timmy Doyle quietly opened the door to his brothers' bedroom and tiptoed in the dark to the lower bunk occupied by his big brother Brian. An eighth-grader, Brian protected Timmy, and Timmy idolized him. His fifth-grade brother, Mick, also lived in the shadow of Brian.

Timmy's sisters, Colleen and Peggy, just did the dishes and got good grades.

Timmy shook Brian's shoulder. "Huh, what?" Brian groggily said.

"It's happening again," Timmy whispered so as to not wake Mick.

"What?" Brian asked as he rubbed his eyes.

"Father Rizzanno rubs my head and grabs my shoulder just like Father Sam used to do at altar boy practice."

"Shit," Brian said as he swung his legs to the floor. Brian led the eighth-grade boys. He was one of the bigger boys, a good athlete, and competent student when he wanted to be. He also headed the altar boys. Because of this, their parents and the church allowed Timmy to start training early. In Timmy's first appearances on the altar, they allowed him to serve only with three other experienced boys. He represented the "dead end" which meant he served on the left side, where he basically did nothing but round out the four and learn the choreography, when to kneel, when to bow, when to stand up. They did not allow him to handle the water and wine cruets or the book for fear he'd drop something.

"OK," Brian said. "Don't go to any more practices or serve any more Masses until I figure something out. And don't tell Mom or Dad. Go back to bed," Brian ordered.

Timmy eased himself out the door and Brian lay back to think.

The following Saturday, Brian and two other ecclesiastical vigilantes met near sundown at the back gate of the cemetery. They wore blue jeans, blue sweatshirts, black caps, and they had smeared dark grease on their faces.

"Just like the Special Forces," Jack commented.

Faced with a locked gate, the boys quickly jumped over the wall. They sat with their backs against the wall on the side closest to the gravel path but behind some gravestones.

They did not have to wait long before Father Rizzano went by on one of his circles around the cemetery. Soon they heard the crunching of gravel again as he approached. When the priest had passed this time, Brian whispered, "It'll be dark enough the next turn," and crawled over to and behind the grossly large monument of the Monahan family, the local undertakers, that sat next to the path. His cohorts followed.

When Father Rizzano, his head down in contemplation, passed the monument Brian stepped out behind him and quickly slipped a large burlap bag from the feed store over the priest's head. Jack and Tim tackled the priest from the back and knocked him to his stomach. The priest's muffled cries, some decidedly unpriestly, soon stopped when Brian stuck a chloroform-soaked rag over the priest's mouth. Even through the burlap it did its job.

They bound his hands and feet quickly, picked up the comatose body, and started down the path.

When Monsignor Kelly arrived back at the rectory at about one a.m., he was surprised to see so many lights on. Usually Father Rizzano left only one light in the living room lit. Kelly walked through the rectory and saw no sign of Rizzano. He looked in the priest's room. No Rizzano. Recalling the priest's habit of walking in the cemetery, he got a flashlight and went outside. About halfway around the path he saw in the distance a bulky statue where a graceful one had stood before. It was the classic statue of the guardian angel with wings spread wide in protection over two small children who played at the angel's feet. Kelly approached slowly. The beam of the flashlight revealed the body of Father Rizzano bound to the statue with strip after strip of duct tape. Kelly gasped. When approached closer he saw a note pinned on the priest's shirt.

"It were better for him if a millstone was hung around his neck and he were thrown into the sea than he should cause one of these little ones to sin." Luke 17: 2

Monsignor Riley put his hand on the priest's neck. Thank God he had a pulse. Then Kelly noticed the smell of the chloroform. The monsignor hurried to the kitchen and returned with box cutters, scissors, and smelling salts. He soon cut the priest down, freed his arms and legs, and laid him on the grass. A few sniffs of the smelling salts had the priest awake but groggy.

Eventually he came to enough to tell the monsignor what had happened.

"Evidently you're paying the price for some one else's sins," the monsignor said after he heard the story. He helped the younger man to his bedroom and into bed. "See me in my office after noon Mass," he said as he left.

The monsignor went down to his office, poured himself a whiskey and water, and sank into his lounge chair.

"Jesus, Mary, and Joseph," he sighed. "What's going on? Good thing we're not back in rural Ireland. They might have used a millstone." With that dismal thought he finished his drink and trudged up to bed.

The next week the church bulletin announced Father Rizzano's transfer back to his home town downstate, to live in the same parish with his aged and ailing parents. The parish wished him well in his new assignment and invited all to a farewell coffee in the parish hall for Father Rizzano after the last Mass next Sunday.

"We should go and say goodbye. He's been nice to Timmy," Brian's mother said when she read the notice. Brian didn't reply.

Technology

"Hey Jim, look at this." Sean tossed a small black box, a little bigger than a cigarette package, on Jim's desk.

"What is it?" Jim picked the gadget up and turned it over in his hand.

"Something you'll want. You're always bitching about cell phones in restaurants. This sucker shuts them off. You and all the people that hate cell phones in restaurants will want one. It's a jammer.'

"How does it work?' Jim asked.

"It sends out radio signals and prevents cell phones in its coverage area from decoding network signals.

"No crap. Where'd you get it?'

"Picked it up at duty-free when I returned from Europe last week. Thought some of our clients might want to license it in the U.S."

"Is it legal?"

"No, not in the U.S., but someday, maybe."

"Let's try it." Sean said. "I'll call your cell phone.

Sean dialed and Jim's phone rang. Sean punched the red button on the small box. The ringing stopped.

"Dead as a doornail," Jim said. "You've got quite a toy here. Somebody could make a bundle."

"At $900 a pop they ought to clean up."

"Speaking of cleaning up we're late for our lunch with Fred and his client. Let's go get some of their money."

Sean slipped the gadget into his pocket as they set off for the City Club.

The lunch was wetter than usual. They had a drinks before and wine with. Then they reached an agreement. That called for a couple of rounds of after-dinner drinks. As the men finished their coffee, a cell phone went off at the next table.

"I thought this fancy club barred those things," Fred said.

"It damn well does," Sean said, slightly slurring his words. "I'll fix that sum bitch." He pulled the box out of his pocket, aimed it over the client's shoulder towards the offending table, and pushed the red button. The noise stopped in mid-ring as the client lurched sideways in his chair. A groan came from his mouth as his head hit the table. He slid heavily to the floor, his hands at his chest.

Silverware and china slid and crashed as the men on either side of him reached down to help.

The man twitched once or twice, but now lay still. Jim felt his neck. No pulse. He held his hand in front of his mouth, nothing.

"My God, I can't understand it." Fred said. "He just had his pacemaker replaced last week."

Sean looked at the black box still in his hand.

The Legacy

My legacy? Mike told you to ask me about my legacy? That's a laugh. He must feel mean. Well, it's about quitting time so if you have a few minutes, sit down in the back booth. That's where Leo used to sit.

I'll have a Coke. No beer for me. Man, my feet are in the fifth decade of serious hurt. Of course, I don't admit to those decades. I still try to pass for fifty-five. A good hairdresser, some makeup slapped on, and a not-too-critical public help. People don't care how old you are as long as you serve them fast and the food's hot.

Most of the breakfast and lunch crowd don't even look at me. More accurately, they look but they don't see a person, just a wait-ress, excuse me, waitperson in a yellow dress taking orders. Number one for lunch, hamburger and fries and number one for breakfast, two eggs any way, toast and hash browns and lots of coffee. Fewer pancakes nowadays—people pay more attention to their health. Yeah, even in this dump.

You're a pretty young reporter. You don't know this area. Used to be a hot manufacturing area but it's all gone overseas. Now we have warehouses to store the stuff brought in from overseas before it's shipped around the states.

My customers, mostly male, work as clerks, accountants, middle managers, and salesmen—tons of salesmen. We get a bunch of truck drivers, too, before they unload or load up. The breakfast crowd don't think they have time to eat at home. I think most of them don't want to. We make sandwiches, to take out for lunch if they want it. Get a bunch for lunch, too. Guess they just have to get out of those offices even though it's only to Mike's greasy spoon. Actually we're Mike's Lunchroom.

The legacy? I'll get there, honey. Gotta give you background. Lemme get another Coke.

Anyway, I work from six a.m. to two, or when the lunch rush ends. Rosa comes in at two. That's her over there. She works 'til eight. Pretty slow at night. She and a cook can handle it. We have two cooks and three waitresses on the early shift. The pay's a joke and the tips aren't much, but Mike's not bad to work for. He doesn't drink and he doesn't hit on you. I make enough to pay my rent and a little besides. He's pretty understanding of an old gal. I've cut my cigarettes down to three or four a day, so he doesn't mind if I go out in back once in a while. A couple of times when I looked really bad off he lets me take off for the AA meeting in the basement of the church in the next block.

Quit squirming around, girlie. I'm gettin' there. Well, I thought I'd retire when I hit sixty-five. Figured I might go down to Florida, live with my sister, maybe work part time. I thought that before Leo.

Who's Leo? A dead man. I used to think he was a nice old guy. He stood about five-foot-four and in his eighties. Looked his age. Sort of wrinkly. But you noticed his clothes, first thing. Didn't look real rich, but neat as a pin. Always had on a jacket and tie. Crisp white shirt. Pressed pants and shined shoes. Always the same clothes but they were always clean. Mike said that Leo must go straight home each day and iron everything. Once in a while he had a different tie.

He spoke soft and had a little accent. He didn't say a whole lot so we didn't know much about him. We figured he lived in one of them little one-room apartments that you find all around here, and ate dinner in his room. He came in five days a week at nine fifteen, after the morning rush. Always ordered the same thing, the number one, eggs over easy, rye toast, hash browns, and coffee. He'd sit in this back booth. Never had any meat. Don't know if that was because of diet or expense. He'd read the paper if he had one. He got 'em off the other tables where people left 'em. He grabbed them quick. It didn't matter what paper. He read them all and every part of 'em—sports, business, fashion, society. Didn't make no difference. After a while I'd bring him the papers people left. He gave me an extra nickel tip when I did that. Always tipped. Figured it out with a pencil. Very careful. Paid ten percent at first and then raised it to fifteen. He figured it on the whole bill, too. Not just before taxes like some of the guys do.

Getting there, honey. Pick up your pencil. One morning he told me he had fixed up a will from a kit he bought at the stationary store and asked if Mike and I'd witness it. I hesitated but then said sure. Mike did the same. We figured he had no friends. A couple of days later he brought in a brown envelope. After breakfast, with only two other people around, he pulled out some papers with blue backing on them with "Last will and Testament of _____" printed at the top and his name written in below. He said he'd sign and we'd sign on a line under something that said we'd see him sign it. We signed a couple of other papers he said he needed to file the will. Leo got out one of those old ink pens and in front of us he signed them all. We signed below. He said thanks and that we'd never forget this. It seemed a strange thing to say but we chalked it up to his foreign use of words.

That happened over a year ago. He kept coming in until about ten days ago. Because of his age we thought that something might have happened but we didn't know where to check it out.

Then last week this slick-looking guy came in about ten o'clock. Dark suit, hat, briefcase, the whole lawyer schtick. Mike told me later that he thought somebody was suing him because of the lousy food. Wasn't that. He wanted to see me. We sat in this booth. He asked me my name and asked to see my driver's license. I don't have one. I told him he just had to take my word for it.

"I have some bad news for you. Leo died two weeks ago."

"I'm sorry but I really didn't know him that well."

"I thought you were related."

"Why?"

"He named you in his will and because of the agreement that you signed."

"What?"

"Yes, he left you his four cats and a letter saying he thought a kind person like you would take care of them."

"Yipes. I don't want them. I'm allergic."

"You can turn them down. I'll take them to a shelter."

"Great. What's that about an agreement?"

"You signed this agreement the same day you witnessed his will."

"I didn't agree to nothing."

"Yes, you agreed to payoff the unpaid balance on his two grandchildren's student loans."

"No Goddamn way."

"Here, I'll show you. You owe Harvard thirty thousand dollars."

"Crap, you say."

"It's a binding agreement. It's my job as the lawyer for the estate to collect on the agreement. By the way, I happened to find out you have thirty five thousand dollars in a savings account. That'll do nicely."

"That's my life savings," I yelled.

"Well, you can pay me or pay a lawyer to fight us when I sue. Think about it."

Then I poured my coffee on him. He's suing me. Too bad it wasn't McDonald's hot. So that's your story, kid. Kindly old waitress befriends lonely old man and gets stuck with four cats and loses her life savings. Now get the hell out of here. I've got dishes to clean up before I go to my second job. I need some retirement money.

The Cottage

Six financially powerful people sat around the table. Outside, the tree leaves gleamed in brilliant reds and golds. A few hundred yards west, the whitecaps broke and rolled onto the white sandy beach. A bright sun and blue sky belied the brisk forty-degree temperature of late fall. It defied belief that this tranquil, bucolic scene lay within a short drive of one of the major industrial and financial centers of the United States.

The six hours of chilly rain the day before had soaked into the ground, leaving no clue except damp earth.

"I hate spending the last fall days inside in these stupid meetings," Kurt, the corporate lawyer said. "I spend all week in meetings and now this."

"Nobody wants to meet," snapped Moira, the committee chair and a vice president of a major bank. "Somebody has to approve new members, so let's get it over with and go relax. That's why we bought these damn places."

The other four members of the committee included Sally, a real estate wheeler-dealer; Fred, head of a large accounting firm; Eric, a surgeon; and Denis, the human resources vice president of a major automobile manufacturer.

"Well, we're not going to relax if this sale goes through," Fred said.

"Look, what's the problem?" Denis asked. "This guy seems OK. Family man. Plenty of money. He owns Roma wholesale and retail liquor. They have stores all over the place. It's not like you have to socialize with him or even see him. We've got a couple of hundred yards of trees between our cottages."

"No question he's got the bucks. I pulled up some financial stuff besides what he gave us. He's rolling in dough. That's not the problem. He's also rolling in family, in more ways than one. He's got eight kids. Five of them married with kids of their own, and lots of uncles and cousins. The stereotypical large Italian family."

"What do you mean?" Moira asked.

"I'm saying that if he moves in, he and all his relatives will overrun this area. I don't want thirty or forty paisanos running all over on the weekend when I'm trying to relax. The next thing, his relatives will buy up the other houses and make this Little Italy. I've seen it before. A bunch of guys running around in dago-Ts."

"That's pretty strong, Fred."

"I'm not done. What about the other family? The one you see on TV and in the movies. We know they're in the liquor business. Do we want that family here?"

"You're out of line, Fred. We can't keep someone out just because of your suspicions. They sound pretty extreme to me," Kurt said.

"Well, that's how I feel. So what do we do, mister attorney'?"

"Under our agreement we've got to approve the new member unless we have a reasonable basis for turning him down. We can't turn him down because he's Italian."

"Why not?"

"First, he'd fight us in court. It'd cost us a bundle even if we won. Second, if you're right and he's connected with the Mafia, we'd get into an area I don't want to go."

"Eric, Denis, any thoughts?" Moira asked.

"Out of my area," Eric said. "I'll do whatever the majority decides."

"Me too," Denis added.

Finally Sally said, "Let me talk to some of my pals in the real estate business and my contacts at city hall. I'll see if I can come up with anything useful. I'll get back to Moira in a few days."

"What do you have in mind?" Kurt asked.

"Nothing. Just fishing."

"OK, you're the nearest neighbor and would be affected the most. Get back to me this week. We have to decide by next Sunday. In fact we'll meet here next Sunday unless I call and cancel," Moira concluded.

The group agreed to leave it in Sally's hands. They went out into the bright sunlight and entered their Mercedes, BMWs, and SUVs and drove to their "cottages" to enjoy the rest of the beautiful day.

The next evening Sally met Francis O'Malley in a ubiquitous Starbucks on the edge of the financial district in the city.

"Hello, Francis. How are you?"

"Still prospering."

"Good. Remember a few years ago you helped a client of mine who had a cash flow problem?"

"Don't remember a thing."

"Ok, Ok. I need someone to help me."

"Let's take a walk."

The two started to walk down the almost empty street, bundled against the cool weather.

"How can I help?"

"I need a property to disappear."

"Where and when?"

"This week. It's a private house in a gated community on the lake."

"Do you own it?"

"No. It's a favor for a friend."

"Gimme the address and I'll look at it."

"The gates are locked. Meet me here at ten a.m. tomorrow. I'll take you by."

Sally picked up Francis on schedule and drove the two hours to her cottage. After coffee they walked down the windy beach so Francis could see the front of the house in question. They walked a few hundred yards past the house and came back on the road in rear of the houses so he could see the house from both directions.

Once they returned to Sally's cottage, she asked, "What do you think?"

"Some cottage. Anybody living in it?"

"No."

"Piece of cake. Where's the nearest fire department?" he asked.

"Twenty miles down the highway. It's a volunteer department so they won't get here too soon."

"Even better. That's $25,000 up front."

"No, $20,000. Ten now and ten after the job. It's my slow season."

"All right."

Sally went into her home office and came back with a travel bag and gave it to Francis. "Here, in small bills. Open it when you're out of here."

"Wow, you mean business."

"Right. I want this done before Saturday. Can you do it?"

"Sure. You certain it's empty?"

"Yes. The owners have moved to Florida. They're there now. Tell me the night you're going to do it so I can travel far away."

"I'll tell you right now. Thursday. Give me the combination to the gate."

Sally gave him the combination and drove him back to the city.

The next day Sally phoned Moira. "Moira, I've talked to a number of my friends in real estate and they don't see a way out. Guess we'll have to let him in or get sued. By the way, the guys in the police department found no connection between him and the Mafia."

"Well, keep working on it. See you Sunday and we'll take a vote. Bye."

"Bye."

Friday at five a.m. Sally's phone rang.

"Hello."

"Sally, It's Moira. The Johnsons' house burned down. I got a call from the fire department."

"Johnsons?"

"Yeah, the sale house next to your house."

"Oh my God. Is my house OK?"

"It's fine. They couldn't save the house, but they got there soon enough to contain the fire and protect the adjoining houses, including Kurt's on the other side. Some trees burned up."

"Anyone hurt?"

"No, thank goodness. No one in it."

"What caused it?"

"Don't know. The fire chief thinks it had something to do with the wiring."

"That's hard to believe in an almost new house. How much damage?" asked Sally

"Almost total. It burned a lot before the watchman noticed it."

"My gosh, what does this do to the sale?"

"Probably kills it, unless the seller's obligated to rebuild. Better check with the lawyers."

Late Saturday morning Moira called Sally again. "Hi, I'm calling all the board members. Looks like we won't have to put up with all those Italians."

"Kurt had that problem, not me. What happened?"

"Apparently the contract lets the buyer elect to get out and he did. Gets his earnest money back. He put up about $70,000. He's going to look someplace else."

"Glad we don't have to fight this out. See you later."

"Bye."

Sally's phone rang as soon as she put it down.

"Sally, it's Francis. I'll be at Starbucks at three for the rest of my money."

"All right. Good job."

Later that day Francis made another phone call.

"Uncle Luigi? It's Francis. How're you? How's Maria and all the kids? Great. Yeah, Mom's fine. She said to say Hi. She's sorry she couldn't make Angela's first communion. She was sick. She said to tell Angela that Aunt Theresa has a present for her.

"Anyway, I handled that house deal you wanted me to take care of. Yeah, the house burned down. I had your real estate agent tell them you wanted your down payment back. Pretty lucky. I know, I know, you didn't want the house, but Maria talked you into it. You Italians act too soft with your women. You give them everything. You ought to be Irish and Italian like me. Glad to help. No, no fee. That's what family's for. I didn't do anything. Honest to God. OK, OK, I don't want to insult you, Luigi. I'll pick my fee up Sunday when we come for dinner. Bye."

Mort Arthur

Mort Arthur was near death. Not "in extremis" as the lawyers might say, but, in his late seventies, he was nearer death than birth no matter how you slice it. Not that he looked his age. Someone, the Army or his mother, had taught him to stand up straight so that when you saw him, especially from a distance, he looked much younger. When he started to walk with his cane he looked more his age.

Mort knew all about death. He had buried Marie, his wife of forty years, some time ago as well as a son and most of his friends. After Marie died he stayed in the house a year, but the repairs and other expenses grew too great. Especially as he had spent most of their savings on trying to get Marie well with chemo. None of the remaining children, a boy and two girls, could afford to help him. Scattered to the coasts, two in the east and one in California, they had their own families to worry about.

He moved into a one-bedroom apartment in a not-so-fancy neighborhood. Still, its location near the center of town meant he could walk to places that interested him.

Life had worked out fine until his stroke two years ago. He felt lucky to suffer only a mild stroke. Thanks to great therapists, he got out of the whole thing with only a weak right leg and arm. He used a cane to help the limp. Left-handed to begin with, he got along OK with everyday things.

Mort had his little routines. Most days he went in the morning to Bergman's, where his investment in one of their plastic cups entitled him to all the coffee refills he wanted for ninety cents. He'd drink, read the papers, wait until people on their way to work left, then fill up one more time for the road. Sometimes he took the coffee home and put it in a thermos for later. Some days, when the shop got busy, he wouldn't even pay the ninety cents. Just go to the urn, fill up, and sit down. If anyone noticed, they didn't say a word. He sat quietly and didn't bother anyone. Many days he sat at the community table and discussed the headlines of the day with the judges, lawyers, and others on their way to the courthouse a few blocks away.

Mort had worked as a plumber, and he was a good one. He was drafted into the Army at eighteen and survived the fighting in Europe. One of his buddies, Steve, also came from Chicago. They went into the Army together, stayed together all through Europe, and got discharged together. Steve was the nephew of the president of the plumber's union in Chicago. A powerful man. While maybe not exactly saving Steve's life in France, what Mort did came close to it, so when they got home Steve helped Mort land a hard to get apprentice spot with the union. Mort worked hard and supported his family but the cold weather got to him. He heard about the building boom in California and the Southwest. Over Marie's objections, he left his job and took the family west.

The move worked well. Construction was mushrooming as the country rushed to get into their own homes. With all the overtime, Mort prospered. Still, he got nonunion wages and had no job security. When the development you were working on finished, you had to hunt for a new job. When they started having children, Mort and Marie decided to stop following the builders. He found a job with a reliable plumbing firm in a small city in southern California. It didn't pay a whole lot, had a poor medical plan, and no savings plan, but the schools were fine and the work steady. That was over forty years ago. The town had grown, so now he found himself a survivor in a city of over 900,000.

Some mornings, depending on how he felt or how long he chatted in the coffee shop, Mort might walk the ten blocks to the courthouse. First he went to the nondescript coffee room in the basement where he could sit and watch the lawyers and court personnel catch a rushed coffee or talk to their clients before a hearing.

He'd ask the clerks he had gotten to know about any good trials going on. If he found one, he'd sit in, but even the supposedly interesting trials seemed very boring, so he usually didn't stay long. Once in a while, he'd hit a time in a trial when the defendant in a criminal case or the plaintiff in a civil case testified and he'd stay. Mort believed he could tell when they lied. He'd make a note of the case name and try to find out later what happened from one of the clerks. The liars usually lost. Hooray for the juries.

Mort saw himself as a peaceful man. He'd always tried to find the middle ground. He'd served on grievance committees in his union. He had even volunteered for mediation training in his town, but he didn't like family cases, and there wasn't much call for a plumber as a mediator.

After he left court, if he felt strong enough, he'd walk the four blocks to the county library. He liked the library. He'd browse and read until he thought it time to go home. There, he read newspapers from cities where his kids lived or that he had visited or wanted to visit. He liked seeing the events in those distant places.

On decent days he'd sit outside at the tables with the steady clients who could not take their bedrolls inside. Some called them homeless, but as one of them explained, they were just between homes. Mort knew many of them, and they knew him, by sight if not by name. Despite their sometime scruffy appearances, many were well read and certainly well traveled.

His library friends included Red, apparently named after his face color, and Red's buddy Bill. Although they traveled together, they had different life views. This apparently created no problem until it came to political discussions. Bill called Red a "knee-jerk liberal pinko" and Red in turn labeled Bill a "right-wing fascist."

At least that's what they called each other when the discussions got heated. Mort, who had lived and raised a family under many administrations, considered himself a middle-of–the–roader despite his union beginnings.

Therein lay the seeds of Mort's tragedy.

One afternoon, after what Mort suspected was an exclusively liquid lunch, Red called Bill's favorite candidate "a dimwit with an IQ of forty who had trouble tying his shoes."

Bill called his candidate's opponent a "stiff puppet who spoke techno-babble." The language and the atmosphere heated up until Bill used a lot of words he didn't learn at church to describe Red's candidate. Red got redder. He jerked Bill's lengthy gray beard. Both men jumped up and faced off. The security guard looking out the library window started toward the front door. Bill grabbed his knapsack that contained all his worldly possessions and swung it in a wide arc toward Red. Mort moved between the two men to separate them as the heavy sack reached the top of its parabola and started down. The forty-pound bag landed like a baseball bat and dealt a pulverizing blow to the right side of Mort's old head.

As if poleaxed, he dropped. Blood gushed from his ear and mouth. His brittle bones had not protected the soft tissue inside the skull. Shocked, both fighters, joined by the security officer, knelt to help the old man.

EMS examined Mort as he lay on the sidewalk. "Looks like the eardrum could have broken, and some of the small bones in the ear," one said to the other.

They felt almost certain that the temporal bone that contained the ear canal, middle ear, and inner ear received a fracture. The clear fluid coming out of the ear could be coming from the brain, but they wouldn't know for sure until they could do a scan. By any guidelines, Mort was not in good shape.

Bill and Red left in separate police cars for the jail at the courthouse four blocks away. Mort left in an ambulance with sirens shrieking and lights flashing. Through no fault of his own, Mort Arthur, the peacemaker, was nearer death.

Another Christmas Memory

Vice president—worldwide sales! I mentally jumped up and down and did one of those semi-lewd dances football players do on TV. And I didn't even have the big job yet. I had just gotten promoted to vice president of U.S. marketing from my job as head of sales for the Western United States, but the CEO told me that I'd get the worldwide job when the present guy, old Joe Cornish, retired.

I deserved the job. I started with the company as a grunt sales-man twenty-seven years ago and worked states with lots of driv-ing—Iowa, Nebraska, the Dakotas. I climbed the ladder: assistant district sales manager, district sales manager, assistant zone manager, zone manager, interspersed with assignments back to Chicago. It's a wonder Mary stayed with me. We met at Northwestern as two rich kids with doctor parents from the suburbs north of Chicago. How'd I get to salesman for consumer products? My goal was salesman, but I didn't want to sell stocks, bonds, or real estate like my classmates. Then this guy who had started a company ten years earlier came to Northwestern to interview. I liked him and he liked me. It seemed to work out.

On my stints in Chicago I picked up enough credits for an MBA. It helped me move along but not make big leaps. Mary and I had two kids in the first five years. We towed them along and they seemed to prosper.

So why did Mary stick with me? Because we both had the same dream of making it big and coming back to Chicago on our own terms and not on the coattails of our parents. Weird but that's what we wanted to do. Maybe some shrink can explain it.

I called Mary. "Foster says I have it when Cornish retires."

"That's gee-rate," Mary screamed. "When?"

"About a year."

"When will we move?'

"Right away. The company relocation people will call you tomorrow. Get your real estate buddy and list the house. It's all programs go."

"What about a new house?"

"I'm going to take a drive up to our old neighborhood in Kenilworth tomorrow and scout it out. After all, the senior vice president of worldwide sales and his bride have to have a prestigious address. The kids need a nice place to come home to."

"Don't commit to anything 'til I see it."

"Don't worry, I'll just drive around and look at the local paper. You come next week and we'll look with a realtor."

"Love it. Let me know what things look like. Bye, dear."

"Bye."

Well, there it was. "Well maintained two-story older home on one acre of land! four bedrooms, three baths, large living room, study, library etc. etc." I couldn't believe it. I looked again.

Yes, four twenty-four Hardbacker Lane. The house that I'd grown up in.

My dad died fifteen years ago, Mom, ten. Both in their seventies. Mom stayed in the house a couple years after Dad died, but it was too big for her. I couldn't afford to keep the house. I had no siblings. My sister died at two.

I couldn't believe my eyes. Talk about completing the circle or karma. I broke my resolve not to talk to anyone when I saw that Joe Wright, one of my old high school buddies, worked with the firm handling the house. He probably never left the area. I called him. He told me that the people selling decided to retire. He worked for one of the big law firms in Chicago. They had bought the house from Mom. Joe told me the asking price. Steep but I could handle it. I told Joe I'd call Mary that night and get back to him.

"Mary, you're not going to believe this."

"What?"

"My old house on Hardbacker's for sale."

"So?"

"I want to buy it. It's some kind of omen."

"You don't want to do this, Andy."

"Yes, I do. Think of all the fun we'll have at the country club with our friends who went to work for their daddy and never left town."

"That's not what I mean."

"What do you mean?"

"Mary Beth."

"My God. I've blocked it for so long it never entered my mind."

Mary Beth was my little sister. She'd died more than thirty years ago, but I'd never forgotten her. I remembered her as well as a five-year-old can remember his two-year-old sister. I still had a couple of pictures of her. She died at Christmas. Someone kidnapped and killed her. We woke up Christmas morning and she wasn't there. Mom and Dad looked all over for her. I remember Mom screaming.

The police came but we had no clues. I learned later about all the searching they did. Mom had some papers with big headlines, but she must have thrown them out because I never found them in her stuff.

Finally, about three weeks after Christmas, they found her body in Lake Michigan. The killer had hit her two or three times in the back of the head with a blunt object. We never got a ransom note or anything that told us a motive. I had a lot of counseling. I remembered only that she'd disappeared and they told me she would not return. We never talked about her at all. That seems strange now. After that year, we never spent Christmas at home. We went to Florida or California. One year we went to Switzerland.

Over the years her kidnapping represented a historical event, like Pearl Harbor.

"Mary, let me think about it. I'll call you back."

I found out from Joe that Otto Wiese, one of the guys on the debate team with me in high school, had opened a psychiatric practice. He lived in the next town. Otto and I got together over a couple of drinks. I told him the whole story and Mary's concern. Otto said that if it hadn't bothered me yet and I had no direct part in it, the relatively happy eleven years we lived in the house before I went to college ought to offset any negatives. But it rested with me. He told me to go with my gut instincts. I did.

We moved into the house in May. We loved it. We connected with old friends from high school and college. Not all of them were nerds or snobs. The job challenged and rewarded me. Old Cornish kept making noises that he might move up his retirement to the end of the year. I liked life. Sure enough, at the board meeting the first week of December, they announced Cornish's retirement and that I'd replace him. All those years of crawling around the boonies had paid off. The kids called with their congratulations. The round of Christmas parties seemed merrier than ever before.

Christmas Eve we went to services at St. Alban's Episcopal Church. At home we had a Christmas drink. "Do you ever think of Mary Beth?" Mary asked.

"Not usually, but right now I do. Let's say a little prayer for her." We did. We finished our drinks and went to bed.

Sometime later I heard noises coming from downstairs. Mary was sleeping soundly. I got out of the bed and went to the hall railing. It sounded like a woman's voice wailing and a man trying to calm her. I started down the stairs.

"My God, oh my God, what happened!" the woman cried.

"I don't know," the man said. "I woke up after my night cap. I'd dozed off. I stuck my head in the kids' room. They weren't in their beds. I went back downstairs and didn't see them. Then I noticed the basement door open. I remembered we had wrapped the presents on the ping-pong table and left some of them there. I walked down into the basement and saw Andy in the corner, curled up, sobbing. He had something in his hand. I didn't see Mary Beth. I hugged Andy. Between sobs he said, 'She wouldn't give me my hammer! She wouldn't give me my hammer.'

"In his hand was the hammer from the tool set. The metal head felt sticky. I found Mary Beth on the other side of the table. She faced downward and the back of her head was bloody. I felt for a pulse and gave her artificial respiration. But I couldn't revive her."

"I'll call 911," he said.

"No, no, wait," Mom said.

"Why wait? We need help."

She had stopped crying and spoke clearly. "They'll take Andy away. I can't lose *both* of my babies."

"We've got to report this. Andy needs help."

"No. If they take away Andy, I'll have nothing. I'll hate you."

"You're hysterical, Mary."

"I've never seen things more clearly. We can't revive Mary Beth, but if I lose Andy too, I'll die."

"What do you expect me to do?"

"You're a doctor. Get your bag. Give Andy a shot to calm him down. I'll think of something."

By this time the dream or hallucination made me curl up in a ball at the foot of the stairs. I heard Dad come back.

"Andy's asleep. What I gave him should keep him out for some time."

My mother spoke in a calm voice. "We can't do anything about Mary Beth, but we must protect Andy. Take Mary Beth's body and get rid of it. Take her to the lake and put her under the ice. While you're gone, I'll mess up the place. In the morning we'll call the police and tell them we've had a break in and kidnapping."

"That's crazy."

"Do it or I swear I'll claim that you did it. Think about what that will do to your practice."

Dad protested and pleaded but eventually I heard him go to the back door. As I sat there huddled at the foot of the stairs, I heard Dad come back in the house.

"I did it," he said in a flat voice.

"Good. I broke a lock from the outside. I messed up a few things, including Mary Beth's room. I washed the hammer and put the toys right. Now give me something to make me sleep, take something yourself. When we get up we'll call the police."

In two or three weeks they found Mary Beth's body in the lake. No one ever solved the case, although one detective kept coming back. Finally Mom and Dad complained to the chief of police, and he told the detective to lay off and let us grieve. My dad kept treating me with drugs and counseling. He tried to wash the memory out of my mind.

I apparently had fainted on the steps. When I woke up, I went into the living room. And I sat on the couch. The dream, or whatever I had, awakened my memory. I remembered the police all over the house for a few days, asking lots of questions. They talked to me but I told them very little. I didn't remember anything. Probably because my Dad kept me doped up. Finally, I went upstairs.

"Are you all right?" Mary asked.

"Yes, I thought I heard something downstairs."

"Anything?"

"No. Go to sleep."

On Christmas day I called Otto and made an appointment. We never spent Christmas in that house again. I told Mary I didn't like it any more.

Bledsoe Flax's Stories

Bledsoe Flax is a type of attorney that you never read about in the papers or see on TV. You can, however, see them in the courthouses of the country representing people whose non-headline cases are the most important cases in the world to them.

As the story says, " Bled loved the law. The idealism that lives in the hearts of most lawyers, before greed drives it into a little corner, still lived in his heart."

Here are some of his cases. I hope you like them and him.

A Real Practice

Heavily burdened, Bledsoe Flax trudged wearily down the darkened hall toward his office. The sun rose about seven this time of year, but it didn't penetrate to the interior hallway. Bled stopped in front of the office of Flax, Nelligan and Associates.

No associates worked here, never had, and probably none ever would. He put down his physical burdens—the coffee, the bagel, the laptop he was trying to learn to use, the briefcase full of files, the separate fat Morgan file, and the *USA Today*. The interior burdens would have to wait. Bled didn't make enough to buy the *Wall Street Journal,* and the local paper's sports section featured nothing of interest. As he fumbled for this key, he remembered when his former partner, Nappy Nelligan, or their professional assistant, Tanya Scott-Jones, had opened the door for him. But neither of them remained.

He had taken the Morgan file home to prepare for the motion set for hearing this morning at ten. If he won the motion, he had a chance of getting a decent settlement. If he lost it, he'd have to go to trial. He didn't look forward to a trial. Bled hadn't tried a case in seven years.

He inherited the Morgan case when his landlord and mentor, Stew Higgins, died. It was one of the few cases not taken out of the office by clients after Stew's death. Bled had no expertise in commercial litigation. Actually, Bled didn't have an area of expertise. They knew him around the Sivart County courthouse as a divorce expert, not because he handled a lot of them, but because of his own three divorces.

Bled represented the typical lawyer you see around courthouses in this country—except the federal court, of course—unobtrusive-looking barristers whose clients came from the ranks of the non-rich and the non-mighty.

Slightly taller than short; slightly heavier than husky; round-faced with a short neck, receding hairline, and large ears; he struck fear only in the hearts of his own clients. Now, if this unassuming exterior hid a razor-sharp mind, you'd excuse the average looks. But alas it did not. It contained a little brighter-than-average brain.

It got him through, at the bottom of the class, a modestly rated law school in a state where few flunked the bar exam. He started practice clerking for free in a storefront office, then moved over to help Stew Higgins with Stew's busy practice for less than a living wage. His only break was that Stew put him on the lease before he died. The modest office occupied a great location in a fine building across from the courthouse. To keep the office, Bled made payment of the monthly rent a first priority after the payments to his ex-wives.

Bled loved the law. The idealism that lives in the heart of most lawyers, before greed drives it into a little corner, still lived in his heart. He got great joy from the cases he handled for Legal Aid. He got a lot of satisfaction from helping someone get their rent deposit back from a greedy landlord.

His prior evening's review of the Morgan file went well until the third beer. The liquid that washed down the special three-meat pizza got to him. He fell asleep, his head on the file. Waking after midnight, he stumbled half asleep into the bedroom, dropped his clothes on the floor, and slept until five a.m. After a morning shower, he decided that adequate preparation required that he go the office to finish his review of the file.

He pushed open the office door, flicked the light switch, and saw the mess on the receptionist's desk. He'd clean that up later, he promised himself. He took the coffee, bagel, and other burdens into his tiny office. Pushing aside the papers on the desk, he put down the coffee and bagel and stared at the blinking light on his phone. Let it go until I finish my notes for the motion, he thought. That decision made, sipping the coffee, he resumed reading his file.

A hour later he'd finished his notes. He felt ready. He threw the empty coffee cup into the wastebasket, grabbed a yellow pad, and punched the button to get his messages.

"Hello, Bledsoe. This is Blair McTree, McTree, McTree & Green. I've got some good news for you on the Morgan matter. I had a few drinks earlier this evening with Judge Peters. He said we didn't have to argue your motion tomorrow. He'll set the case for trial next Tuesday, and we can argue it before we start. Thought you'd like that. Call me if you want to settle. Bye."

Bled dropped his head onto his desk top, a habit he had recently developed when problems struck.

"Good news??" he yelped. "I've spent hours getting ready. I've got a good argument. He agreed at the club? I didn't agree. What the hell?"

The old boy network of Sivart County had just bitten him. He'd complain to the judge about the one-sided procedure, the judge would agree and give him a hearing, but not without a lecture about wasting the court's time.

"I can't get ready for trial in a week. We're screwed. Another catastrophe."

The prior two "head on the desk" catastrophes had happened five days apart only two weeks ago. First, Nappy left. Nappy, short for NapthaAnn (don't ask) Nelligan, was a bright, idealistic lawyer who wanted to help people. Despite the name on the door, she rented space from Bled and started to build up a practice. At twenty-eight she had been married five years to a computer nerd she met in college. Then, about six months earlier, she got a divorce. She didn't ask Bled to handle it.

One morning she walked into his office and said, "Bledsoe, I've been upset since my divorce. You must have noticed. I may have to take my life in a direction away from the law. I'm going to go away and think about it. I'll stay in touch." Then she walked out. Bled had dropped his head to his desk.

Five days later Tanya, also divorced, came in and said that she planned to leave the following week. Another head-desk meeting. He tried to talk her out of it, threatened, cajoled, pleaded, but the next Friday she cleaned out her desk and left.

Bled had the three-meat pizza with margaritas that night. Juggling with temps and the help of some of his lawyer friends and their staffs, he kept the major fires, of which there were few, under control but felt himself sinking fast. He missed Nappy and Tanya. He needed them. They made a team.

He punched the button to listen to the rest of the messages. They included five clients asking why they hadn't heard from him, five requests for money, two long-distance services offering deals, one ex-wife, and one call from his mother asking why he didn't call on her birthday. Tanya used to remind him. Still furious at Blair McTree, he called him and left an unprofessional, hysterical message. At nine he'd call Morgan and discuss settlement options. He wanted to pace, but his office, only three strides long, didn't allow for pacing.

Finally he settled down and went to the secretary's desk to sort the mail. Thank God for the shredder. It gave him a sense of power.

The door opened. There, smiling like a couple of clowns, stood Nappy and Tanya.

"We're back," Nappy said.

"You're saved," Tanya added.

"I see you're back. Whether I'm saved we need to discuss. I'm almost nuts. What's going on?"

"After our divorces we both felt very unhappy. We talked a lot and then started meeting after work to help each other out. Then we fell in love."

"Who with?'

"Each other."

Bled started towards his desk. "Don't," snapped Nappy. He stopped.

"So we went out of state to get married. We've got more good news."

"Spare me."

"We've snagged a big client. We're now the general counsel of the Association to Legalize and Promote Alternative Forms of Monogamous Weddedness, ALP-AFMW for short."

"For short?"

"Yeah. Who wants to say all that long name?" Tanya said.

"No, no, a thousand times no," Bled said.

"I agree," Nappy said. "Besides, I took their $10,000 retainer."

Bled's head hit the desk hard. His body shook.

"Is he crying or laughing?" Nappy asked Tanya.

"I don't know."

Bledsoe's Big Case

Bledsoe Flax, NapthaAnn Nelligan, and Tanya Scott Jones sat in Bledsoe's office deciding what to do with the $10,000 retainer that NapthaAnn had received from the Association to Legalize and Promote Alternative Forms of Monogamous Weddedness (ALP-AFMW). Despite Bled's reservations, they decided they'd take the client and Nappy could keep the money.

Nappy said she'd pay the back rent on the office space and keep the rickety group together. Bled planned to pay her back his share when he could. The women convinced Bledsoe to accept the money by pointing out that the office foundered under its debt and had only one case of substance, the Morgan case.

"OK, OK," Bled finally agreed. "Just remember that it's my office. NapthaAnn, you just rent space. I'm in charge here."

NapthaAnn and Tanya looked at each other and tactfully did not smile.

"We can act as counsel for ALP-AFMW, but tell them to change the name. The acronym's terrible. Maybe they can have a contest. Come up with something."

The money let them keep the doors open while Bledsoe struggled to find enough clients to support himself. When the lawyer he had officed with, Stew Higgins, died last year, the clients, unfortunately, went to other lawyers.

"Tanya, see if you can get the correspondence caught up. I've been blind-sided in the Morgan case. Blair McTree had a few drinks with the judge at their club the other night, and the judge moved the pretrial and trial to next Tuesday. Morgan's due in here in half an hour to review the case. Considering they haven't offered us anything, we'll likely have a short meeting."

After the women went out, Bled leaned back in his chair and sighed. He wished he hadn't promised Nappy he would not bang his head on the desk when he got frustrated. He'd started the habit a couple of weeks ago after both Nappy and Tanya had walked out on him, leaving him alone. It cleared his head and focused him. Besides, it felt good when he stopped, one of the few pleasures left to him.

The client arrived on schedule. She came in. More correctly, she manifested herself. She was beautiful. Just over six foot tall, she was willowy, slinky, striking, all of them. Ebony hair outlined her oval face. The hair waved at the forehead and fell in soft curls on the side. She had a subtle pleasant scent. A black and red dress accented her beauty.

Her appearance stunned Bledsoe. He hadn't met her before. Previously, Morgan had dealt solely with Stew. Win or lose, this case amounted to the highlight of Bledsoe's career.

Of course, the visit also marked Morgan's first time to see her counsel. She showed no outward reaction of what she thought of the slightly-taller-than-short, slightly-heavier-than-husky lawyer with the round face, short neck, receding hairline, and large ears who greeted her. She politely extended her hand in greeting.

"Please sit, Ms. Morgan. I'm happy to meet you. As I told you on the phone, we've had a surprise. We may have to go to trial next week, but I haven't given up on a settlement. I've gone over your file a number of times, but could you just tell me again what happened?"

"Fine. By the way, call me Cynthia. I'm Cynthia Morgan. I went by Morgan when I modeled in New York. I kept my professional name when I came back home about ten years ago, when the teeners started to get my jobs and my mother became ill. She's since passed away."

"I'm sorry."

"Thank you. Well, due to my experience, VanDorff's women's store hired me to model and sell clothes. They sell mainly high-priced, haute couture clothes. I liked the work and did very well. I received generous commissions and I modeled some."

"What happened?"

"About eighteen months ago, the exact date's in the file, the owner, Klute VanDorff, called me in and said they had a plan to change things on the upper-end of woman's clothing selling, and he'd have to let me go."

"Just like that?"

"Just like that."

"No other reason?"

"None."

"Unfortunately, Cynthia, this is an 'at will' employment state, and unless you have a contract, they can fire you at any time."

"So Stew told me, but he also said he'd try to help me."

"It'll be difficult. We have to find some other element. Some type of harassment or discrimination. Did anything like that go on?"

"No. Not at all. Most of my fellow workers were women and the men all had good manners. Actually, Mr. Flax, because of my height and physical appearance, I scare most men. It has its good side, but it limits social life."

"Hard to believe," Bledsoe murmured to himself.

"What? I couldn't hear you."

"Could be a relief. Please call me Bledsoe or Bled."

"I did hear something later, though. I told Stew. You should find it in the file."

"What?"

"There's a huge swing in the fashion business. The United States is the fattest country in the world, and the industry's pursuing the pleasingly plump market, the fashionably fat clients. The women with mature figures have grown tired of wearing dowdy clothes, so the designers, including labels like Bali and Vanity Fair, decided to target the well-to-do, full-figured women with money."

"How big—pardon the pun—how big a trend is this?"

"Very big. Reportedly over twenty-six billion dollars last year."

"Holy smokes, but how does that help us?"

"There's more. After they fired me, I had lunch with a friend who's an assistant manager at VanDorff's. She told me she heard that they fired me because of complaints about me."

"That's not going to help. Sounds like they've got cause."

"No, you don't understand. Some of the fully figured complained that my presence gave them a complex when they came into buy clothes. My figure put them off. It made them uncomfortable. They said if they didn't get rid of me they'd shop elsewhere."

"That's terrible. Couldn't VanDorff reason with them?"

"Apparently not. A group of the biggest buyers, in both senses, confronted him at his office. But even that's not the worst."

"The worst is?"

"Mrs. VanDorff spoke for the group."

Without her there, Bled would have hit his head on the desk. He thought the action unseemly in front of a client. Then a thought struck.

"Wait. It looks like there's more than economics at work here. Maybe the little green monster."

"That's ridiculous."

"Maybe so, but more importantly, maybe we don't have enough defendants or maybe we have the wrong ones.

"What do you mean?"

"We can sue the women who pressured VanDorff and VanDorff for conspiring to have you fired. You had an oral contract and they forced a breach. Malicious interference with contract or something. Let me do some research. It's a theory, but I think it has legs." Bled bounced in his office chair and smiled.

"Mr. Flax, Bled, I'm not vindictive. I'd just like my job back and back pay. If you can get that for me, I'll be very grateful."

"I can't promise anything, but let me see what I can find to support my theory. I'll try to set up a meeting with McTree and Van-Dorff Friday or Monday. This ought to get their attention. We may not have to go to trial. On your way out, give Tanya the names of all the women who may have attended that meeting. Thanks for coming in. I enjoyed meeting you." Bled really meant that last part.

Tanya gave him the list of women at the meeting. "We've struck gold," he shouted when he saw the names of the mother of Blair McTree, his legal nemesis, as well as the wife of the trial judge on the list. "This'll rattle their cage. Tanya, pull up the civil conspiracy complaint form on the computer and name all the women on the list as defendants in the first draft. I'll fill in the specifics this afternoon after I get back from the county law library."

Bledsoe did not hit his head on anything.

At nine-thirty Tuesday morning, the beautiful, tall, elegant Cynthia Morgan, with her short, aesthetically challenged attorney at her side, went through the metal detectors at the county courthouse to the admiring gazes of the male security personnel. The female security officers ignored Bledsoe. The defendants had stiffed Bled's attempt to set up a prior meeting. In his briefcase, Bledsoe had his silver bullet: an amended complaint adding an additional count of conspiracy and naming as defendants, among others, the defense attorney's mother and the wives of the store owner and the presiding judge. He also had a motion requesting Judge Clink to recuse himself from the case, and legal memoranda to support his positions. Bledsoe didn't think the judge would allow his amendment at this late date, or recuse himself, but he thought he'd shake them up and get the other side to talk. With Cynthia at his side, he strode into the courtroom with an aura of confidence.

When the case was called, Bledsoe presented his motions. "Too late, Mr. Flax. Too late and you know it."

The judge saw the motion to remove him from the case. "You're on the verge of contempt, Flax."

"Mr. Flax."

"What?"

"I'm an officer of the court. I'm Mr. Flax, Counselor Flax, Attorney Flax."

The judge sputtered; Cynthia smiled.

While this exchange took place, Attorney McTree and his client VanDorff read their copy of the documents. McTree blanched when he saw his mother's name. VanDorff winced when he saw his wife's name.

The judge calmed a bit. "Your motions are denied. Let's pick a jury."

"Just a minute, Judge," McTree said. "My client wants to have a brief talk with the plaintiff and her lawyer. We need to clarify something. May we have a few minutes?"

"Don't you start wasting my time, too. Let's get this fiasco over. Ten minutes, no more."

Bledsoe, Cynthia, McTree, and VanDorff went into the empty jury room to talk. It didn't take long for Bledsoe to convince McTree and VanDorff that even if the mother and the wife were not defendants, he intended to call them as witnesses.

At two o'clock the door to Bledsoe's office popped open and, like the Pillsbury Doughboy, Bledsoe popped in. He held a bottle in each hand.

"Tally ho. Champagne for everyone." He obviously had refreshed himself before his entry. Nappy rushed out of her office.

"What happened? Aren't you on trial?"

"Not a bit, my little legal eagle. I've been at La Petite Bistro having celebratory lunch with my happy and comely client."

"Tell us all."

"Well, the threat to haul all those amply endowed prominent citizens into court got their attention. After they frothed and fumed and the judge threatened to hold me in contempt, we worked out a settlement. It appears that old VanDorff's thoroughly smitten with Cynthia."

"What'd you work out?"

"First, VanDorff really wants Cynthia around as some eye candy. The missus was the one who wanted her fired."

"No surprise there," Tanya said.

"VanDorff loved the idea of us 'forcing' him to take Cynthia back. The wife can't blame him. Once we got that established, it was easy to get him to agree to pay all back wages with interest and a little something for Cynthia's trouble. He moaned and groaned, but I also got him to pay our fee. We're rich."

"How'd ya do that?"

"Actually, I didn't. We got stuck, but after I kept pointing out to Vandorff how unhappy his wife would be to miss her charity meetings standing around waiting to have her deposition taken and appearing at the trial, McTree talked him into it. I suspect that McTree may have adjusted his fee."

"The job?"

"Oh sure, she gets to go back and with a written contract this time. They never doubted her great sales ability. Most of the customers love her."

"But she's still slinky, elegant. She's always going to intimidate some women."

"Well, that's mostly not true. Most of them envy her but admire her. To the extent that presented a hurdle, we worked it out."

Nappy smelled something. "Come clean. Tell us the whole deal."

"Well, it turns out that Cynthia's not completely happy staying so skinny now that she's not modeling, but her metabolism's stuck on thin."

"Yeah," said Nappy smelling female abuse. "So what?"

"So the VanDorff company's going to send her to a fitness spa where she can work out and go on a controlled high-calorie diet until she puts on a few pounds."

"That's cruel and inhuman."

"No. She wants to do it. If it doesn't work or she doesn't like it, she still gets to keep her job."

"Bledsoe, you're an idiot."

"No, a genius. A peacekeeper. A paragon of the bar. A creator of innovative solutions, with money."

With that declaration, he made the last push with his thumbs on the champagne cork, and the office looked like the locker room of the Super Bowl winner.

As they sipped their second paper cup of the bubbly, the phone rang.

"It's for you, Bledsoe. Sounds like Cynthia. She probably changed her mind."

"Bite your tongue, woman. "

"Hi Cynthia. No, you're welcome. we're just reviewing the case. Haven't changed your mind? No. Good." He made a face at Tanya.

"What can I do for you? A week from Saturday? Let me look." Bledsoe put the phone on his shoulder and broke into a fatuous grin. "Yes, that's fine. Looking forward to it. Talk to you soon. Congratulations again."

He put the phone down and continued to look sappy. "Now what's happened on this weirdest of all days?"

"Well, my friends and fellow inmates," Bledsoe announced with raised paper cup, "It appears Cynthia's the incoming president of the local chapter of the ex-models club. She wants me to escort her to the inaugural dinner dance. She wants her friends to meet her champion."

Tanya spit up her champagne, some of it coming out her nose. Nappy fell into a chair in a spasm of hysterical laughter.

"Hey, knock it off. I have feelings, too," Bledsoe grumbled. Tanya recovered first. "Sorry Bled. She's a beautiful woman. Have a good time."

"Thanks. Where can I rent a tux?"

"Try Magnum rentals," Nappy said through her tears. "I understand they'll throw in a pair of heels for you for free."

"Throw this," said Bledsoe as he tossed his paper cup of the champagne towards her.

The Naked Truth

Bledsoe eased his little-heavier-than-husky frame through his office door about 9:15. No rush. Things had gotten very slow since he settled the Morgan case, and his new friend Morgan got her modeling and sales job back at VanDorff's high fashion clothing store. And cash to boot.

Morgan had tasked him to escort her to the dinner dance when they installed her as the president of the local ex-models association. She had introduced him around as her champion, and that resulted in a few calls but not much business. His modest stature, chunky frame, and big ears offset her endorsement.

"You've got a message from Blair McTree," Tanya Scott-Jones—the office manager, professional assistant, and all-around doer—announced.

Blair McTree was a hot-shot Ivy league lawyer at the city's most powerful law firm, where his father was the senior partner. McTree represented VanDorff, the defendant in the Morgan case, and McTree played his role in the city legal establishment to the hilt.

The two lawyers had nothing in common with each other except their dislike of the other.

"He wants you to meet him at eleven at the City Club for coffee. Said he had a case in court 'til then. If you can't make it, call his office.

What in the world's this about, Bledsoe wondered. I've never even gone to that place. Guess I can't lose anything by going, and I don't have anything better to do. Do I need a tie?

Bledsoe, due to his nature and practice, ranked way ahead of the curve on casual dress in the legal profession. Slacks, usually khaki, open-necked shirt, and jacket completed his normal uniform. Most of his clients dressed the same way. He did keep an extra pair of pants, a couple ties, and a blue blazer in the office closet in case of an emergency call to court. At five to eleven Bled entered the City Club in his blazer and tie.

"I'm here to meet Blair McTree," Bledsoe announced to the petite receptionist.

"Down the hall to the third door on the right," she directed.

Nice smile, Bledsoe thought.

Bledsoe opened the door and saw McTree, the only occupant of the room, seated next to the widow with papers spread out on the table, leaving barely enough room for a silver coffee pot and a basket of rolls.

"Bledsoe, come in, sit down," McTree said as he swept up his papers. "Have some coffee."

The friendly greeting made Bledsoe's defenses go on red alert.

"Thank you."

"Look Bled, I know that you're busy."

Ha, Bledsoe thought.

"So I'll get right to the point," McTree continued.

"OK. Can I have some coffee?"

"Help yourself. Have a roll. You impressed my dad with the way you handled the Morgan matter."

"Um," Bledsoe picked up a pecan roll and waited for the other shoe to drop.

"He has a proposition."

"And it is?" Bledsoe asked, stuffing the roll into his mouth.

"You know that we represent most of the major companies in the area."

"Yeah, I know it. Get to the point, or did you ask me here to tell me what a hot-shot you are and what a dork I am?"

"No, no. Relax, Bled. I want to offer you a legitimate business proposal. We get a lot of requests by the powers that be to handle personal matters or represent their employees, friends, relatives, and the like."

"So," Bledsoe said, pouring himself some more coffee and taking another pecan roll.

"Most of the cases amount to a pain in the ass. Usually they think we should do it for free so we waste an associate's billable time, or it's so small that we lose money handling them. Frankly, some of the cases we don't want our name associated with. But we've got to help them or we will lose the big money."

"Look, I'm sorry for your problems, but what has this got to do with me?"

"We want to refer some of these matters to you. You can handle them cheaper than we can and still make money, so we both benefit."

"There's got to be a catch."

"Nope. No referral fees, no connections. Most of the clients will pay a fee to you. While we won't guarantee anything, we'll see you don't get dinged."

"Let me think about it," the still dubious Bledsoe said as he poured a little more coffee."

"Well, normally I'd say OK except that we got a case we want you to look at today. We've set up a meeting this afternoon. You can use the money."

"That's it," Bled said getting up.

"Sorry. Really, my dad checked around and he's truly impressed by how you handle unusual cases, and this one's unusual."

Bledsoe mentally reviewed his cash flow situation—abysmal— and sat back down.

"What's the case about?"

"The college-age daughter of an officer of one of our big clients, Rocker Industries, has a slight problem."

"What kind of problem?"

"I'd rather have her tell you directly. She's a nice kid, a freshman at West State. You'll like her. She and her dad will be at your office at three this afternoon. If you don't want to take the case, tell 'em."

"I'll talk to them but no promises," Bledsoe said eyeing the last pecan roll.

"Agreed."

The men shook hands. Bledsoe stuffed the last roll into his side pocket, hoping it would not get full of lint. "No use letting it go to waste," he said to McTree as he walked to the door.

At five to three Bledsoe shoved the crossword puzzle into his lower left hand drawer, swept the crumbs of his desk, plopped a yellow pad into the middle of it, and scattered a couple of letters around. He was ready for his three o'clock appointment. His cramped office barely had room for his desk and two chairs for clients.

He heard a knock on the door and Tanya, the office major domo, ushered a middle-aged man and a petite girl into the room. Bledsoe registered surprise at her size. He thought McTree said she was in college.

The man, of average height, weight, and coloring, wore an expensive gray suit, white shirt, and blue tie. He looked like a McTree client. The girl looked different. She stood about four feet eleven, slender to skinny with a long blond pony tail, bright blue eyes, and clear, creamy skin.

"Mr. Casey?" Bledsoe inquired.

"Yes, and this is my daughter Kathy."

"Nice to meet you both. Please take a seat. Blair McTree says that you have a situation that I might help you with?"

Bledsoe tried to hide his extreme curiosity about what kind of problem this prosperous-looking man and his tiny daughter had that the big-time McTree firm couldn't handle.

"Mr. Flax, I'm the chief financial officer of Rocker Industries," Casey said, trying to establish his importance.

"Please call me Bled. You know that corporate law's not my bag, so I'm curious as to why McTree sent you to me," Bled said, leaning back in his chair and trying to look as important as Casey.

"This isn't a corporate matter. It's personal, and McTree told us that you're very good at handling cases in a discreet manner. We need discretion."

Bledsoe didn't know how to take that, but you don't run off a client who could obviously pay his bills.

"Suppose you tell me the problem."

"I'll let Kathy tell you."

Bledsoe turned his chair to focus on the diminutive figure in the other chair. For the first time he noticed her well-developed—but not bulky—forearms, shoulders, and legs. "What's up, Kathy?"

"I'm in trouble with the police."

"Drink? Drugs?"

"Nothing like that." She got out a handkerchief and dabbed her eyes. "It's worse."

Not pregnant I hope, he thought, keeping his eye on the elfin figure.

"I was arrested for indecent exposure."

What the hell? A preteen girl? "OK, start at the beginning."

The girl composed herself. "I'm a freshman at West State University."

"Wait. How old are you?"

"I'm eighteen."

"But . . ."

"Yes, I know I look younger. I've always been small. That's what has gotten me into gymnastics and cheerleading. That's part of the problem."

"OK. Go on."

"Well, I made the cheerleading squad at West State U. The only freshman ever to do it. And that started my problem."

"Congratulations I guess. What happened?"

"The cheerleading squad hazes new members. I'm the only new member on the squad this year, so I suffered the hazing alone. Some of the girls on the squad got mad that a freshman made the squad, so they decided to get me."

"Stupid," Mr. Casey rumbled.

Bledsoe moved his legal pad to the center of his desk to start taking notes.

"The school has a tradition that the night before the homecoming football game, some of the frat boys streak across the west quad."

"The school allows this?"

"Not really. But they sort of wink at it. It's usually over fast, and not many people paid attention to it until couple of years ago when some of the religious groups complained. The school nabbed a few streakers and handled it within the university system. Unfortunately, this year some townspeople complained to the police—but we didn't know that."

"Let's get back to your story."

"The senior cheerleaders decided that a woman should take part in the streaking, and the cheerleaders, me specifically, should lead the way."

"You agreed?"

"No, Mr. Flax. You don't know how mean a group of girls can get and the pressure they can bring. I really, really didn't want to do it, but they said if I didn't, they'd not only prevent me from cheerleading, but they'd keep me out of all groups on campus. I believed them." She started to weep.

"Kathy, stuff it," Mr. Casey said. "Finish the story."

Not too sympathetic, Bledsoe thought.

"Kathy, do you want some water or a Coke? Anything Mr. Casey?"

"Some water, please," Kathy said.

"Nothing for me," Mr. Casey added.

Bledsoe went out and came back with water and a Coke for himself. He felt sympathy for Kathy on an intellectual level. No one had ever asked him to join a group that had an initiation. Bledsoe plunked down in his seat.

"After they threatened me, they said that they'd take me to the start in a bathrobe," Kathy continued, "and meet me at the other side with another robe, put me in a van, and hurry me off."

"So how did things go awry?"

"They didn't. The run started, I dropped the bathrobe, ran like mad behind the boys, got covered up at the end, and hopped into the van as planned."

"So why do you need me?"

"The next day the police called me and asked me to come to the police station."

"You went?"

"Yes."

"Alone? Why?"

"I didn't want anyone else to know. I wasn't sure what they wanted."

"Did they arrest you?"

"I don't think so. They treated me really nice. A policewoman took me into a conference room and showed me a film of the streaking. They said some group had taken pictures and brought it to them and insisted that the streakers be prosecuted."

"You're sure they didn't arrest you."

"Pretty sure. The policewoman said that they were still talking to the university and that I should get myself a lawyer. She gave me a card and said that she'd call me later."

Bled didn't know much about Reedsburg, the small town that was home to West State. It had a conservative reputation, and he'd heard about the usual town-gown conflicts, but he'd also heard that the town fathers let the school police itself. However, as the school grew, certain groups in the town had grown more upset at the students.

"Give me the policeman's card. I'll call her and get back to you tomorrow." On that they parted.

After they left he looked at the card. Sgt. Heidi Burger—didn't mean anything to him—but then he had never had any clients in Reedsburg. Of course he didn't have many anyplace.

Two days later, Bledsoe walked into the police station in Reedsburg. Originally a farming community, it was now a college town and retirement center.

"Sgt. Burger please. I have an appointment."

"Heidi," the desk man yelled toward a door in back of him.

A few seconds later, a woman with a paper cup of coffee in her hand appeared through the door. Her five-foot-six height, blonde hair, blue eyes, and rounded figured made her a bigger version of Bled's client. He presumed that the Sergeant had noticed the resemblance. She seemed a good representative of the Germanic roots of the community.

At Berger's invitation they settled in a bare conference room, and she gave Bled a paper cup of industrial-strength coffee.

"Sarg, what's going on? This is a college prank, nobody hurt. Why go after my client?"

"Relax, counselor. Nobody here's out to get Kathy." Bled noticed the use of the first name. "But you've run into a buzzsaw of local politics. The police chief and the city attorney feel pressure to clamp down on the 'goings-on' at the college. Normally we'd handle this administratively, but they're getting a lot of urging to prosecute from the CLAN."

"The Klan!" Bled exploded. "They've been out of business around here for a zillion years. What the hell?"

"Not that Klan. It's C.L.A.N. Christian Ladies Against Nudity."

"Who in the world are they?"

"We had a hell-and-brimstone preacher through here about eight months ago. He ended up pulling together a group of fundamentalist Lutherans, Catholics, and Baptists to stamp out evil wherever they find it."

Heidi left the room and came back with fresh—sort of—coffee and some leaflets. "This will give you an idea of the group. They're against gambling, pornography, alcohol, and whatever. Actually we don't have much of that here except for alcohol. The CLAN's an ad hoc subcommittee of the pornography group."

"Amazing." Bled sipped at the fresh coffee. It was hotter than, but just as bitter as, the cup he had before.

"Anyway, these ladies knew about the annual streak and tried to get the college to ban it. The college said they had sent out all sorts of material over the years 'prohibiting' the run but to no result. The event seemed relatively impromptu and happened at different places. The police don't have enough people to cover the whole campus even if they wanted to."

"That didn't end it?"

"Nope. The ladies are righteous. They got somebody to stake out the campus and take pictures of the streak, took the pictures to the city attorney, and demanded action. Unfortunately, Kathy's easily identifiable."

"And the male streakers?'

"Oh, they've got them by the balls, to use a phrase," the sergeant said with a straight face. "But because of her sex, Kathy's a special target of the CLAN. We, or I, tried to talk them out of it—got them down to indecent exposure—but the judge and the city attorney are elected, and they don't want to be targets of a religious crusade in the next election."

"Got a copy of the code?'

"Made you a copy." She slid some papers across the table. Bledsoe read in part, "A person commits the offense of indecent exposure if he exposes his genitals and is reckless about whether another person is present who will be offended by his act."

Doesn't look too good, he thought. "Have they decided to prosecute?"

"Not finally. The school still wants to handle it internally. They scheduled a meeting for next week to make a final decision. The CLAN and the school people will go. Maybe you should be there, too."

"Let me talk to my client and see what she wants to do."

As Bledsoe read the code in the police station, a small buzzer sounded in the lower recesses of his brain. Bled didn't have brilliance, but God had gave him a very retentive memory, which got him through law school and through the bar exam. Something about genitalia . . . no, some legal theory. What was it?

Back in the office, Bled attacked the large stack of outdated state, county, and American bar publications tossed in the corner of the conference room. He wasn't looking for law as such but an anecdote in one of the sections devoted to strange or humorous (supposedly) law cases. Finally he found what he'd sought. He read it once, twice. A smile sliced across his face. He grabbed his Martindale Hubbell Law directory, turned to the Florida listings, and thirty minutes later he spoke by phone with attorney Marabou Smith of Sandbeach, Florida.

"Nappy, can you come in?" Bledsoe asked. "I need your help on this case."

NapthaAnn slid into a seat in Bledsoe's office with a yellow legal pad in her lap. She thought his request unusual. Bled usually was above, or beyond, help. "What's up?" she said.

"I've got a case that needs—really needs—a woman's touch."

"Do what I can."

"Bledsoe told NapthaAnn about Kathy's case and his meeting with the policewoman, then he stopped.

"Is there more?" Nappy said.

"I'm a little embarrassed."

"Now that's an image."

"Well, it's about a woman's sexual parts."

"For God's sake, Bledsoe, you've married women three times.

"Yeah, but we never discussed the equipment."

"Get over it."

"I'll try. Well, this attorney down in Florida got an indecent exposure case thrown out by arguing that the woman's genitalia are inside the body and therefore not 'exposed.'"

Nappy stopped taking notes. "You're not serious."

"Yes."

"And a judge bought it."

"Yes."

"And you're going to try it?"

"We're going to try it," he corrected. "With a little different twist. I'm going to try to keep it from going to trial. That's where I need your help. Here's what I want you to do."

With the help of Sgt. Heidi Burger, Bledsoe got himself included in the meeting with the city officials, the school, and the CLAN. Bledsoe and NapthaAnn arrived fifteen minutes before the scheduled meeting time with an easel, five large poster board exhibits, and a pointer.

Sgt. Berger introduced Bledsoe and Nappy to City Attorney Wagner, Chief Schwartz and the Misses Berg, Krause, and Kelly, representatives of CLAN. Or maybe they were the total membership. The ladies looked stern and thin to gaunt, depending on your view. Each head of gray hair was pulled back into a bun. Hatchet-faced came to Nappy's mind. Perhaps they also belonged to the Christian Ladies Against Eating, mused Bled. Well, they'll live longer than I will.

"Mr. Schwartz, Mr. Wagner," Mrs. Berg began unbidden, ignoring the others at the table, "we've told you that we're fed up with the immoral activity on the campus, and we want something done about it. The school can't or won't act. We want these people prosecuted to the fullest extent of the law. And you, Mr. Wax, or whatever your name is, your client's the worst. A disgrace to womanhood, the Blessed Virgin, Joan of Arc, Mother Teresa, Martha Washington, Martha Stewart . . ." she sputtered as she ran out of models of perfection. All the time, Mrs. Krause's and Kelly's heads bobbed up and down in agreement.

Geez, what have I gotten myself into? Bled thought. "Just because you find something offensive doesn't mean it's against the law," Bled replied. The city and school officials had heard it all before and were happy to stay out of it.

"That hussy you have as a client ran naked across the campus. She's guilty of a least indecent exposure," Mrs. Berg continued.

Bled had a very difficult time imagining his petite, pretty client as a hussy. But then he wasn't sure what constituted a hussy.

"No, she's not," Nappy said.

"Look counselors, we're going to proceed against your client. You can say what you have to say at the trial," the city attorney said.

"You're wrong," Nappy interjected. "Look at your code. To be guilty, my client had to expose her genitals. She didn't do that."

"Well, I never," sputtered Mrs. Kelly.

"You're nuts," Chief Schwartz said. "We have pictures of her running naked across the quad."

"That may be, but you forget your basic anatomy," Nappy said as Bledsoe put their exhibits up on the easel covered by a cloth. "Let me refresh you."

"I think that I'll get a drink of water," Bledsoe said as he eased out the door.

Nappy pulled down the cloth revealing a large, colored, anatomically correct drawing of the female genitalia.

"Shocking!" Mrs. Berg bellowed.

"Disgusting!" Mrs. Krause chorused.

"Filthy!" Mrs. Kelly keened, then collapsed.

"She's swooned. Get some water, " Mrs. Berg blurted.

I guess if you call someone a hussy you can say someone swooned, Nappy thought for no good reason.

"Put the cover back on that thing," Chief Schwartz ordered.

"What's the point of this?" Attorney Wagner demanded.

"The point is that the woman's genitalia is internal, so our client did not publicly display hers, and hence no public indecency."

"Ridiculous, outrageous," the attorney said. "Besides, no judge is going to buy that or let that into evidence."

"I don't know. Dr. Ruth and a few other sexologists we're going to bring as experts may use it when they testify. Hope you got plenty of hotel rooms around, because the press will send a lot of people to cover this story."

The CLAN members had recovered enough to shout threats at the city officials if they didn't do their jobs as they stalked out the door.

"This is nonsense," Wagner said to Flax, who had returned.

"I don't think so. Why don't you talk about it and let me know."

"I'll let you know the trial date, that's what I'll do. Take that pornography out of here."

Frantic phone calls went back and forth the next week by and between the city and college officials, the mayor, and the local judge. They had no further conversations with the CLAN. Finally, the mayor's stand that he wasn't going to turn the town into a national news story coupled with the judge's statement that she refused to preside over an anatomy lesson carried the day. They instructed the city attorney to cut a deal. Consequently, no charges were filed against Kathy. She agreed to do twenty-five hours of community service. The university agreed not to mention the incident in her file.

The male streakers pled guilty, paid fines, and were ordered to do fifty hours of community service. The university noted the incident in their files. The university agreed to increase its efforts to prohibit streaking and also put all the cheerleaders, except Kathy, on a semester's probation.

Mr. Kelly received and gratefully paid a substantial bill from Bledsoe and NapthaAnn.

Bledsoe burned the exhibits.

Pokémon Justice

At one thirty the door to the office slammed open and Bled shot into the waiting area. "Tanya, quick, where's the petty cash box?"

"In the top file cabinet drawer. Why?"

"Emergency." Bledsoe opened the wooden Pantagas cigar box, a throwback from who knows when.

"Six dollars and fifty-eight cents! Is that all we've got?"

"What you see is what we've got. This isn't the McTree firm, ya know. What's up?"

"The truck drivers' strike started this morning. No more deliveries. Take this money and run down to the store and get every Twinkie it'll buy."

"You're nuts. "

"No, they have a very short shelf life. We've got to get them and put them in the fridge.

"I thought the Twinkie defense applied only to nutty defendants, not nutty lawyers. Get them yourself. Besides, you have a client waiting in your office."

"Who?"

"Willie Joe Smith, your nephew by marriage and divorce."

"The squirt."

"The client."

Bledsoe walked into his office. Across from his desk sat a blond-haired, intelligent-looking young man about twelve years old. Bledsoe and Willie Joe had crossed swords before at family gatherings. The young man was reading *Harry Potter and the Chamber of Secrets*.

"Any good?" Bled asked.

"Bestseller."

"Would I like it?"

"You wouldn't understand it."

"How's your aunt?"

"Your ex-wife? Having the time of her life."

"Yeah, thanks. What can I do for you, Willie Joe?"

"I want to sue my school."

"The dream of a million children. What for, teaching not up to your standards?"

"Help me get justice."

"For what?"

"They took my stash."

"Stash?"

"My supply, my inventory."

"You a drug dealer? I can't help you."

"No idiot, my Pokémon cards. I buy and sell them, and they stole them."

"Stole? Whatdaya mean?"

"I had my collection in a book in my bag when I walked down the hall. A security guard saw it and took it. They won't give it back."

"Sounds to me that you shouldn't have had them in school, and they had a right to take them."

"Maybe so, but they should give 'em back."

"Did you ask?"

"Two weeks ago, and they've stiffed me. Not only that, but the same guy has taken five or six more collections I know of. He doesn't even wait until they're out sometimes. If he sees the cards in your bag, he grabs it."

"Look, I'd like to help you, but I'm really busy."

"Yeah, really," Willie Joe sneered.

"Your parents should handle this."

"My dad called the school. They said they couldn't find them, and that ended that, as they saw it. Dad doesn't want to call again. He's a wimp. You're a wimp too, but you're a lawyer wimp. Call them up."

"Go buy some more."

"You don't understand. I'm a dealer, not a collector. These were my prime assets, my stock, my inventory. I had $2,000 worth of cards in that folder. I want to sue them for damages."

"Two thousand dollars. That's a lot."

"I told you, I'm a dealer. I specialize in rare cards. Some cards go for up to nine hundred dollars. I had a couple Charizards that go for seventy to one hundred dollars. When a guy's trying to make a deck, he'll pay above market," Willie Joe pointed out.

"Well, you might have some basis for a suit, but I don't work for free," Bledsoe said, still trying to get rid of Willie Joe. "Sorry."

"Didn't think you did." Willie put his book bag on Bledsoe's desk and started rummaging. He pulled out, and piled on Bledsoe's desk, a binder, a math book, lots of loose papers, an apple, and a candy bar. Finally a brown manila envelope appeared in his hand. "How much?"

Got to get rid of him, Bledsoe thought. "One thousand dollars up front, one hundred fifty dollars an hour."

Without hesitation Willie pulled out stacks of bills neatly separated by rubber bands into piles of ones, fives, tens, twenties, and fifties. He started counting. When he got to eight hundred, he reached in the envelope again and continued counting. When he got to one thousand, he pushed the money over to Bledsoe, put the rest back into the envelope, and shoved the envelope and all his debris back into the backpack.

Bledsoe gabbed a yellow pad and a pencil. "Give me the details. The date and time it happened, the name of the guard, and the principal for starters."

When Bledsoe felt he had all the basics, he sent Willie Joe on his way with a promise to make some phone calls and get back to him.

"You'd better," Willie Joe warned as he departed.

"Tanya," Bledsoe said, handing the notes to her. "Open a file on this and see if you can get someone in the principal's office at Willie Joe's school for me. Oh yes, call the school district's security office and see if a Fred Decker still works there. He's an old drinking buddy of mine."

"Him and a hundred other guys. Did you get a retainer?"

"Let me talk to him if he's there."

"Did you get any money?"

"Why do ya ask?"

"Because I think you did, and we need to put some in the petty cash and the bank."

Bledsoe emptied both pockets and gave her a bundle of cash. She counted out eight hundred dollars.

"Is this all?"

"No, I kept a little back for expenses."

I bet, Tanya thought. But she didn't push it anymore. Bled needed to have something in his pocket.

"The dance, the dance. How'd the dance go?" Tanya sang out when Bledsoe made it into the office Monday morning at nine thirty.

Bledsoe Flax, the slightly-taller-than-short and slightly-heavier-than-husky attorney, made his first appearance in his office since he had escorted the statuesque and beautiful Cynthia Morgan, his grateful ex-client, to her inaugural ball as the president of the local chapter former models' club.

Bledsoe flinched at Tanya's almost attacking style. Still, he knew he'd have to give a report of the date to NapthaAnn and Tanya. It reminded him of when he had to report to his mom after one of his infrequent dates in high school.

"Great." He smiled broadly to reinforce his words. He really meant it. "Cynthia thinks that I have real potential as a dancer."

"She means you can't dance," Nappy said.

"Don't talk like that," Tanya interjected.

"Toss me the phone book, Tanya, I'm going to take a few lessons to brush up."

"Brush up? How can you brush up on something that you don't have?" Nappy continued. "Really, Bled, you're out of your league. Just because you won a case for Cynthia, don't get delusions. What makes you think those tall beauties have interest in you?"

"Damned if I know, but at my height I saw a lot of great backs and a lot of great fronts of backs."

"Calm down, Bledsoe," Nappy said.

"Look, the dance had a lot of business potential. Cynthia told everyone how I got her job back for her and some money to boot. I handed out a bunch of cards. Cynthia told me, in a brutally frank manner, that my physical appearance would help me get some business from the models who were tired fending off male lawyers, accountants, etc. who thought themselves God's gift to women."

"Some asset," Nappy said.

"That's enough from you, Nappy. I'll tell Tanya about the dance at lunch and you have to guess about it."

"Getting to business," Tanya said. "Bled, you got a call from your client and nephew, Willie Joe, who wants to know the status of his suit against the school to get his Pokémon cards back."

"First, it's not a suit yet. I'm setting up a meeting with the school district to see why we can't get them back. Did you ever get my buddy Frank Decker in the school district security office?"

"Yes, he's still there. Here's the number. He said to call him."

Bled took the number into his office and called Decker. He gave him the name Jim Collins, the security officer who took his nephew's cards and now claimed he didn't know what happened to them. They agreed to meet at four in the afternoon at Dusty Gulch, one of their regular watering holes. Then Bled went into Nappy's office.

"What's up, Nappy? You were pretty hard on me."

"I know, Bled. I'm sorry. My practice isn't going anywhere, and things aren't working out between Tanya and me.

Tanya and Nappy had entered into marriage after their first marriages failed.

"Well, maybe the Morgan settlement will bring us all some business. Sorry about you and Tanya. You know you all sort of jumped into that relationship after your divorces. God and my three ex-wives know I'm not too good in my relationships, but I'll gladly lend you a shoulder."

"Thanks, Bled. Let me think some more. I may take you up on that offer. And maybe I was so hard on you because I'm a bit jealous of you finding Cynthia."

"That's nothing. I think she's just a good friend. You pointed out our differences—short, husky lawyer, tall, glamorous model. See you later."

At about five minutes after four Bledsoe put down his Heineken bottle and cracked the last peanut in the basket. Following custom he tossed the shell on the floor to join its relatives.

"Yo, Josh, bring me some more peanuts," he yelled at the bartender.

"Yo, Bled. Get'em yourself. Just because you won a case, don't get uppity. Geez, it's bad enough that you're drinking Heinekens and not your usual."

Bled pushed himself away from the round table for six, which he occupied alone, and grabbed another basket of peanuts from the bar. The Dusty Gulch Saloon was one of the four drinking places that shared his business. They were his equivalent of the fancy clubs the Ivy League lawyers hung out at to drum up business. He called the Dusty his University Club. Bled also belonged to the City Club (Bob's Tavern), the Metropolitan Club (The Court House Inn, which got extra business from the legal community as their receptionists could honestly say they went to the Court House when they took a long lunch), and the Athletic Club (Brian's Sports bar). Each of these "clubs" had at least one community table that sat six to ten, where Bledsoe Flax, attorney at law, was an honored drinker and commentator on the public scene at least once a week. Attendees and graduates of these floating public meetings included people from all walks of life, including journalists, councilmen, court clerks, and tradesmen of various descriptions. Unlike the membership of the more famous aforementioned clubs, the participants at Bledsoe's hangouts were all male.

Here, Bledsoe had met many of his clients—not the high rollers one met at the more prosperous places, so the best that Bledsoe could hope for was a one-shot representation and a paid bill. But that suited him. Not that Bled drank much. At least not anymore.

The three ex-wives had moderated his activities and shrunk his bankroll.

Bled celebrated while he waited for the drinking buddy from the school district security office who said he had found something for him. He had started his second Heineken when Frank pushed through the door.

"Sit down," Bled invited. "Have one on me." Seth handed Frank a beer in its cozy. Two people sat in the back room and only one man sat at the nine-seat bar, so Bled felt free to talk business.

"Find anything?" Bled asked.

"Yeah. Your boy Collins has an interesting story."

"How so?"

"He's an ex-cop from Chicago with a completely clean record in our files."

"What's so interesting about that? Sounds like a dead end."

"I'm an investigator, Bled. I wondered why an experienced cop wanted to work school security when our local police force begs for experienced people at a lot more money."

"And you discovered?"

"He's hiding something. He knows the police require more information than the school district, and he wanted to avoid that."

"How does that help me?"

"That doesn't, but I did. You forget that I come from Chicago. I called one of my Irish cousins still on the force. Seems your boy left under somewhat of a cloud. He played on the fringes of a big shakedown scandal a couple of years ago. The district attorney made a deal with some of the officers they couldn't nail. He and several others took early retirement."

"What kind of shakedown?'

"They stopped recent immigrant drivers who spoke little English. They told them they'd lose their green cards if they got a traffic ticket. They usually settled the deal for cash."

"Nice guys, picking on the Hispanics."

"Nope. Croats, Bosnians, and Serbs, the whole new wave from Eastern Europe that moved into Chicago. People who feared the police at home."

"Any way to prove it?"

"Nah, but I did pull up some copies of news stories. Here, I brought them. I underlined the name Henry Star. He got convicted."

"What's the point?"

"Star partnered with Collins when the investigation started. They had separated and the investigators couldn't put Collins at the scene of any particular shakedown, so he got off. Nothing about any of this on his application."

"Thanks my friend, I think I can use this with the school district. Have another beer."

Other customers had started to drift in as the business day ended. The shuffleboard got busy. Two of the men noticed that Bled's conversation did not seem as intense and moved toward the circular table.

"Bled," said Red Foley, a tall red-haired man, "I hoped I'd find you. I called your office and found out you weren't in, and took a chance you might come here. Meet Phillipe. He has a problem."

"Don't we all?" Frank said.

"A legal problem."

"Sit down," Bled invited. "I'm still celebrating and I can still stand another round. Josh, draw us a pitcher of beer. Phillipe, do you mind talking to me here?"

"Nope," Phillipe said.

Josh plopped down a pitcher of beer and four glasses and only sloshed a little on the table. Bled filled the glasses and raised his glass, "Good luck to our friends, confusion to our enemies," he toasted.

"Bled, you've got to stop drinking with those Irishmen at the Court House," Frank said.

As the men clinked, Phillipe's glass shook and he spilled beer on to the table. "Geez. Watch it. You a spaz?" Bled said.

"Yes, sort of," the man said quietly. Bled's face dropped.

"Sorry," he said softly.

"That's why we're here," Red said.

"I'm not a doctor."

"Phillipe, tell him."

"I work two jobs. I clerk at a grocery store during the day. Do a lot of grunt work. Stack, carry out, and the like. I hurt my hand on the job and had to have an operation. After the operation my hand had this tremble. I didn't have this problem before."

"And?"

"The lawyers for the doctors and hospital made me an offer of settlement, but it's not fair."

"They rarely are, but why don't you think so?"

"Because they won't compensate me for the loss of income from my night job."

"What's that?"

"I'm a tattoo artist."

"No crap."

"No crap. Nobody wants a tattoo from someone whose hand shakes. I tried to go back to work, but when I start on a customer they see my hand shake and leave. Some even cuss at me. The shop I worked at won't let me come in anymore. I've lost over three-fourths of my income."

"What's your lawyer say?"

"He said to take what they offered. Besides, he just took a job with the federal government, and I don't like the lawyer he turned it over to."

By this time people filled the bar, and the group at the table almost shouted to be heard. Bled gave Phillipe his card and told him to call for an appointment and he'd see what he could do.

Bled picked up the clippings Frank had brought him and edged his way through the happy hour crowd. Settle one nutty case and you get another, Bledsoe thought. Well, it's a living.

He went to his office to call and set up a meeting with Collins. With the information Fred Decker gave Bled, it didn't take long for him to convince Collins to mend his ways. A short time later Willie Joe had his Pokémon cards back, and security guard Collins applied for a transfer. He cited as the reason the need to work closer to home.

Bledsoe and Jovanna

"Two!" I yelled as I tossed the wadded-up yellow legal sheet toward the basket attached to my wastebasket. The basket had arrived a couple of years ago, a gift from my deceased mentor, Stew Higgins. The paper ball landed on the side of the rim, teetered, and fell off. No basket. Crap, just like my teams in the NCAA pool. Hell, just like my practice—teetering on the edge and falling off to zip.

Actually things had not gone too bad financially. NapthaAnn and Tanya had landed the retainer from the Association to Legalize and Promote Alternative Forms of Monogamous Weddedness (ALP-AFMW), and I made good fees from Morgan-the-model case and the case of the little cheerleader accused of indecent exposure. Still, these amounted to one-shot deals, not enough to build a practice on. After I paid the rent, utilities, and the women got something to live on, little remained for me. Besides, the money's not my main problem. I'm rudderless.

"'Nite, Bled," Nappy yelled a she stuck her head through the partly opened door.

"'Nite."

"Whoa, you look even worse than usual. What's up?"

"Nothing. Just the usual downer when you come off a case," I said.

"That happened last week. Come on, let's go get a pop."

"Can't."

"Nonsense. I've seen your calendar. You've got no social life."

Overlooking the adverse but accurate comment on my social life, I reluctantly pushed my self out of the chair, slipped on my wrinkled jacket, and followed Nappy down the hall.

Mid-level, middle-aged, successful lawyers—those that made up the bulk of the bar in our city, or any city for that matter—gathered at Bob's Tavern as an after-work place. At six fifteen they already crowded in. We eased our way toward one of the two small tables in the back. The tables for two usually filled up last, as the drinkers had not yet start to pair off.

"What do you want, Nappy?"

"Pint of Harp."

I moved to the second row of bodies at the bar and yelled at Trinka. "Two pints of Harp." No use complicating the order. "And run a tab."

I got the beers back to the table with minimum spillage and took a long pull at the glass.

"Feel better?"

"No. I'll take more than a little beer."

We drank in silence for a while.

"Look at me, Bled," Nappy said.

I kept staring into my beer.

"Dammit, look at me."

I raised my eyes but not my head.

"I've worked with you for a while now and seen you in bad moods, but usually you still talk. So talk to me."

I ran my finger around the top of my glass. "Nothing to say."

"Hogwash. Either talk to me or some $200-an-hour shrink."

"Some choice."

The silence resumed.

After a while she said, "I'm getting two more beers. When I get back you had better start talking."

While she fought her way through crowd, I finished my beer and felt a little more relaxed.

Nappy plunked the two beers on the table. "OK, talk".

"Not much to tell. I just realized I'm middle-, almost-middle-, near-middle-aged. No family, divorced three times, marginal at best law practice. No girlfriends or prospects, short, fat—God damn, it's depressing."

"Whoa, Whoa. You're not short, you're sort of average height, you're not fat, you're husky. At least you have a practice doing something you like to do. I can't rationalize the divorces, but they're behind you, and you have lots of friends."

"Acquaintances, not friends, and don't give me that glass half-full baloney. See this pint? It's half empty and it's getting more empty, just like my life," I said as I took another gulp.

"Bled. You need a girlfriend. What about you model friend, Morgan?"

"A friend, just an occasional date. Too tall and beautiful for me."

"Sgt. Heidi what's-her-name you worked with on the cheerleader case? You seemed to get along."

"Liked her. Had one date with her but she lives too far away for steady dating. Besides, her handcuffs hurt."

Nappy's eyes snapped wide open. "What?'

"A joke. Relax."

"Church?"

"Been there, done that."

"Hobbies?"

"Don't collect, run, bike, jog, swim, or do anything that causes me to sweat."

"Bled, you're almost hopeless," Nappy said putting her hand on mine.

It felt good. I slipped my hand out from under hers.

"Thanks," I said.

"Let's go," she said.

I paid the tab and followed her through the crowd. I admired the view of her trim back in her blue lawyer's suit. I walked her back to her car. She turned to me to say goodbye, and I kissed her. Not hard, just right.

She smiled. "'Nite, Bled. Hope you feel better. See you tomorrow."

The next few weekends NapthaAnn and Tanya set up series of parties to which they invited me. I enjoyed them, and they all had one thing in common. An excess of female lawyers, doctors, teachers, therapists—you name it—attended each one. Apparently the women had pored over their address books, and the books of all their friends, for single, soon-to-be single, or those who just wished they were single, women. None of them seemed interested in a short (average height), fat (husky), economically challenged lawyer.

Except for Jovanna. An attractive blonde, she was a tennis instructor at the Wood Creek Club, a local upscale place. I think the big-time McTree law firm had memberships there for all their partners. Jovanna had come to the United States ten years ago from Prague on a tennis scholarship to West State University, the site of my recent case. She apparently still retained a European respect for the legal profession. Most of the men she met were members of the club, off-limits for dating. Or they were involved in tennis for a livelihood in some way and, as I later learned, she had had enough of that.

Asking around, I found out that after college she had gone on the pro circuit for about five years until she realized she was not going to be the next Capriati or Hingis and came back to the States to start a career as a professional tennis teacher.

Jovanna, attractive and more quiet than most, showed up at every party. While she spoke very good English, once in a while she lapsed into an accented word or two that underlined her uniqueness.

For some reason, maybe because she was a foreigner and I was certainly a foreigner among the successful, good-looking men, we found ourselves together more and more. As a good Czech, she enjoyed good beer. She didn't abuse it, just enjoyed it, as Europeans do.

Before the fourth party I asked Nappy if Jovanna was coming. Nappy said yes, so I went over to our fancy food center and bought a good Czech Pilsner beer.

"Thank you, Bled. You're very thoughtful," she said when I produced it at the party. That little incident seem to bring us closer together.

At first we mostly talked about my practice. She had a quick mind and asked insightful questions. We also talked about tennis, of course, and I picked up tennis magazines at the library to learn the vocabulary and names of current players.

When I heard about the next party, I called Jovanna, picked her up, and took her.

We had a pleasant time. After, as we walked up the stairs to her apartment, she said, "I can't ask you in, Bled. I have a roommate and I have a lesson very early in the morning."

Disappointed, I said, "That's OK," not meaning it. I couldn't ask her to my place. It was a mess.

I reached over and eased her towards me. She was about my height and we fit together very nicely. I thought I'd like to do more of that. I kissed her goodnight.

"How about dinner next Saturday?" I found myself saying when my mouth was free.

"A real date? Without all those other people?"

"Yes."

"Fine, let's do it."

I picked a spot that was a mix between a Czech winery, a wine restaurant, and my usual beer-and-pizza place. It turned out that it had a decent menu. I had a steak and Jovanna had *gulas* and *knedliky*, goulash and dumplings, that she said resembled the food at home. A bottle of *cervene*, red wine, did nicely for us both. She explained the words to me. Her healthy habits moderated my eating and drinking.

Our return home repeated the week before, with a pleasant, brief parting at her door. We agreed to go out again the next week.

The morning before our date, I started cleaning my apartment. I could see an all-day job ahead of me. Where do I start, I mused. I got the largest container that I could find, plunked it in the middle of my kitchen, and started dumping everything in sight in it. Old pizza crusts, boxes, bags, magazines, plastic spoons, forks. What a bunch of junk. I got everything visible dumped into the trash can and opened the refrigerator to start on it. God, what a mess. It was only half full of partially full containers, bottles, jars, and bags. And of course beer. I sighed and grabbed a can, and sat down. One plus of dating Jovanna was that I had learned about great Czech Pilsner beer. More expensive than my usual local stuff, but worth it. I took my second suck on the bottle when the doorbell rang. Who the hell? "I'm coming."

I opened the door and saw two angels, my office companions, in sweat shirts, blue jeans, tennies, hair in bandanas, with pails, mops, and brooms. It was more than a social visit. I loved it.

"What's this?" I asked.

"Home aid," Nappy said. "We heard you mumbling about cleaning up the apartment and we knew you had a date with Jovanna, so we put two and two together and figured you needed serious help."

"Nah. I can handle this."

"In a pig's eye," Nappy said. "We've been here. If there's anything to knock thoughts of romance out of Jovanna's head, it's this place. We're here to remedy that. We have a few more people coming, so point us to the washer-dryer and the cleaning supplies, if any, and get out. Quick, before we change our minds."

I grabbed my jacket, briefcase, and newspaper, emptied the beer bottle down my throat, and moved out the door.

"Don't come back until after four and call first," Nappy yelled after me.

Within the hour the women had the bed stripped and the sheets dumped into a pile along with some questionable-looking linen from Bled's closet. They were soon joined by all of Bled's washables from from his bathroom, dresser, and closets.

"Tanya, bring me any kind of tongs you can find in the kitchen," Nappy yelled from the bedroom. When she had the tool in hand, she knelt down and looked under the bed. Then, using the tongs, she pulled out three separate articles of clothing that had apparently been there for a while and tossed them with the washables. She started a separate pile for dry-cleaning items.

Nappy and Tanya finished the coffee they had brought, and after cleaning it thoroughly, started a fresh pot in Bled's Mr. Coffee. About ten o'clock the doorbell rang and Fred, Bill, Kay, and Patty arrived equipped with cleaning supplies, a case of beer, sandwiches, and other snacks. After they finished cleaning the refrigerator, and after a thorough scrubbing, they filled it with beer and food.

Nappy divided the group into bedroom, bathroom, kitchen, and living room teams. Those who felt an early need for support before starting the task popped a beer, as the group started on a task only slightly less daunting than cleaning the Aegean stables.

"I'm glad my mother can't see me doing this," Fred said. "Every time she comes by, she complains how sloppy Bill and I keep our place."

A couple hours later the six grabbed drinks and sandwiches from the fridge and plunked down in any open area they could find in the living room. They surveyed the two piles of dirty clothes and linens.

"God, bachelors live in filth," Nappy said.

"Remind me why I'm doing this," Fred said as he sipped his beer.

"For Jovanna," Nappy responded.

"For love," Kay said.

"Oh, crap," Bill intoned. "For sex is more like it."

"Cynic," Patty chided.

After lunch the group stuffed the wash and dry-cleaning into the separate bags that Bill had brought from the local cut-rate cleaners. They carefully chose a pair of slacks and the least objectionable shirt and one set of underwear and socks for Bledsoe to wear that evening.

"That plus what he has on should hold him until the cleaning comes back," Nappy said.

When Bill and Kay got back from the cleaners, the others had finished the other rooms and sat in the living room with the rest of the beer.

"Not spotless but livable," Tanya said. I wonder how long it will last?"

"It should make it until Bled's date tonight," Nappy said.

"OK," Bill said. "I'll put the receipts from the cleaning on the fridge. Let's get out of here."

The group picked up the trash bags, pails, mops, and brooms, and left.

❖

The sight I saw when I got back to the apartment overwhelmed me. It had not looked that good when I moved in. I called everyone to thank them and left lot of messages. Everyone was out.

I picked up Jovanna as scheduled. It went well. I remembered some of my manners and had read up on the recent results from the women's pro tour to make small talk about that.

I selected a restaurant near my apartment so I could leave my car in my parking space and have an excuse to walk back there. When we left the restaurant we strolled hand-in-hand toward my place. The weather felt soft. As we approached my place I said, "Jovanna, I couldn't ask you up before because my place was such a mess." I told her about the cleaning job our friends had down. "Come on up for a coffee or some more wine."

Jovanna hesitated.

"Bled, I don't think so."

My heart sank. Had I completely misread our relationship? She saw the dismay on my face.

"Something has come up." she said

"A new boyfriend?"

"No. I'm going back to Prague."

"Why?"

"My mother's ill. I'm the only unattached child. It's terminal, and I don't know when I'll return."

"I'll go with you," I heard myself say.

Jovanna smiled. "It's a lovely thought. Silly, but lovely."

"When will you go?"

"Next Tuesday."

"Why so soon?"

"It's not really that soon. I wanted to tell you sooner but waited until I had it all scheduled. You're a fine man, Bledsoe. I hope you find someone, but I don't think we should get more involved now. It will just make it harder for us both. It's simpler if we end things now."

For the first time in a long time, I felt real emotion. I felt close to loving Jovanna. I'm sure my face sagged. I looked at my feet like a schoolboy. My hands fidgeted.

Jovanna put her hand under my chin and raised my face until I had to look into her eyes. "Thank you, Bledsoe," she said as she kissed me. With that she turned and walked away.

"Wait. I'll drive you home."

"No thanks. It's not far," were her last words to me.

I watched her until she turned the corner. I went slowly into the building and into my clean apartment. I started in the living room and walked slowly from room to room tossing slowly and deliberately every loose pillow, magazine, blanket, and towel on the floor. I went into the kitchen and found a six-pack of beer left and took it into he living room. I jimmied off my shoes, dropped into the center of the sofa, opened the beer, and sat staring at the dark TV set.

About the Author

Jack Rosshirt is a retired attorney who spent over twenty years in the international petroleum business, with emphasis on Afirca and the Middle East. He has lived in Tehran, Iran, Nairobi, Kenya, and Copenhagen. Prior to that he served in the US Army Counter-Intellingence Corps. He is a graduate of the University of Norte Dame and its Law School.

He uses his insights into a variety of political, economic, cultural and social philosophies gained through his travels and negotiations with international business and foreign governments to add background and flavor to his writings.

Jack and his wife of 50 years have raised five sons and are the grandparents of seven grandsons and one granddaughter.

In addition to writing, Jack has handled pro bono litigation and mediation. He is an avid tennis fan and certified tennis official.

Kenyan Quest

Jack Rosshirt

Jack Rosshirt has written a book that takes you into the African interior to uncover a secret that has been begging for discovery for more than half a century.

A retired Texas oil executive, a World War II Italian concentration camp guard, a reformed IRA terrorist-turned nun, and an Austrian neo-Nazi all sit down for dinner at a Catholic medical mission in the Chalbi desert in northern Kenya. How they each came to be there, why, and the deadly results is the intriguing story of *Kenyan Quest*.

To order a copy of

KENYAN QUEST

Name _____

Address _____

_____

$14.95 × _____ copies = _____

State Sales Tax
(Texas residents add 8.25% sales tax) _____

Please add $1.50 postage and
handling per book   _____

Total amount due: _____

Please send check or money order for books to:

Jack Rosshirt
3413 Foothill Ter.
Austin, TX 78731

To order additional copies of
RETURN TO DUBLIN

Name _____

Address _____

_____

$11.95 × _____ copies = _____

State Sales Tax
(Texas residents add 8.25% sales tax) _____

Please add $1.50 postage and
handling per book _____

Total amount due: _____

Please send check or money order for books to:

Jack Rosshirt
3413 Foothill Ter.
Austin, TX 78731

Printed in the United States
83106LV00002B/196-333/A

9 781934 541005